Chimerical Escape

*GENUS GLOSSARY IN BACK OF BOOK

Chimerical Escape

by DAVID TALON

Senior Editor
Carolyn Bredschneider

Chief Editor
Gail Miles

Senior Publisher
Steven Lawrence Hill Sr

ASA Publishing Corporation

 ASA Publishing Corporation
An Accredited Publishing House with the BBB
<u>www.asapublishingcorporation.com</u>

The Landmark Building
23 E. Front St., Suite 103, Monroe, Michigan 48161

Copyrights©2018 David Talon, All Rights Reserved
Book Title: Chimerical Escape
Date Published: 09.03.2018 / Edition 1 *Trade Paperback*
Book ID: ASAPCID2380762
ISBN: 978-1-946746-37-5
Library of Congress Cataloging-in-Publication Data

This book was published in the United States of America.
Great State of Michigan

A Publisher Trademark Copyrights page

Chimerical Escape

by DAVID TALON

Origin - Infertile Conception

Mammals as a whole have become infertile for an undiagnosed cause. The solution is "oyle." Created out of the blood of willing reptiles by their intent to heal their furred allies.

This alternative acts as a reproductive restoration of the body, hybridizing a whole new biology of reptile and mammal: gargoyle.

Yet those who opt for the cold-blooded oyle lose sanity as the unstable fluid pulses through their vasculares. Now, the once sentient minds instinctively rely upon the physiological need to feed . . .

Present - Atrophied Generator

Forjah, a vulpine dog of the last generation of mammals, has attained survival for a miraculous duration of time. This dog has been acknowledging the existence of gargoyles by doing all possible to avoid them. Though his body will forever be incapable of procreating, all value has been drained from his vitality, leading to a personality of apathy.

After concluding their academic finale, Forjah does not seek out a new goal. Not even the opening of a new recreation complex, *Escape,* which is offering a desirable salary for everyone hired. Astonishingly, no applicants have been offered as much as an interview, while this vulpine is un-willfully convinced to apply himself. The succeeding night however, he receives a call . . .

Despite the danger of gargoyles looming over *Escape* as newly appointed kart racing operator, Forjah has found contentment in the recreation complex. The schedule of operation is under diurnal light to avoid the nocturnal prowl of the enemy. For it is after hours when the mammal-reptile hybrids thrive.

If not for a spontaneous ailment, Forjah would fathom the risk of being exposed under nightfall. Yet when his mind enters this ill state, all guard is dropped while in the wilderness. A wilderness not so devoid of hybrid predators . . .

SCENIC 1

First Beginning

"Witnessed here is a memory only to be retained by the races of scale and feather," announces the feminine voice, communicating over our ears and through the comm system across the data wave.

"As the mammalia reach their extinction, their reminiscence will only be contained physically by the enemy expected to be their sanctification." The statement reflects my current and exact feelings. I am to be in the finale of our genus, a dog who is to never be forgotten, yet only because I have never been remembered.

"Leave a specified legacy. You are in full acceptance that you are discontinued as a species. You will not be leaving behind a generation as your forefathers, yet leave a historical imprint none-the-less."

"Let it be this way. I willfully accept the greater purity I invest into the end, the easier my passing will be." My warm-blooded hind paws pass from polished tile to a wooden stair ascending to the portable stage where the MC waits aside the podium, bearing the ribbon wrapped scroll I feel forced to accept.

"May this, the finale era of mammals, extend beyond its extinction. All preceding us have been triumphant in attains their education climax, yet in a state no other can visualize apart from us, here we trek with a most unique perspective. I planned ahead with my certified skills."

Trident voices are heard to my side while I trace my pointed digital pads over the stone wall we are passing aside. "Machinery attracts me in many forms, engines especially."

"I am more in focus to the present," I concur. "One cannot reach the future without first triumphing in the present." I philosophically attempt to hide how I care nothing beyond now.

"Just visualize, Forjah!" My cougar companion initiates," If I can acquire the right scrap, I can piece together an engine of steam power."

"I admire your retrospective despite my limited understanding," I admit. "Let me know of my capabilities to assist you."

"Starting research is the priority in that goal, no matter how independent." I pass a pleasing grin to a near exposure of my vulpine jaws. I am always pleased by the joy of my loved ones, as they are the only positive source to my entirety.

In the overshadowing moment, I could make a suggestion or inquire for one. My puma friend takes off along the wall in a startle to my lack of reaction. Halting before its end at the rusted gateway, he pulls a sheet from a mounted box where he positions it directly where my trailing paws meet it.

"You haven't turned in an application, have you?" he presents against my ignorance.

"No desire to."

"Have you even glanced at the salary offered?" the feline boasts with a gaping maw. "Everyone has applied for Escape . . ."

"Yet none have been hired," I reaffirm, while glancing to the newly mounted sign atop the gateway."

"The pay rate is right here. Have you not seen it?" His beastly claw tracks out of its sheath to fall over the number, bringing a grunt from deep in my throat."

"Numbers mean little to me. I also have no experience qualifying for a reaction complex, let alone such a business opening when gargoyles are on the prowl for our blood.

"Which is why," he thrusts the slip against my chest insisting I fill it out, "we have little time remaining in the day." His statement is genuine as I glance to view the sun making its descent distantly behind the skyline."

As if attempting to cool the heat built up by the agitation he has instituted, I withdraw my ink needle before turning my tail, obstructing his view. Sighting only my title and contact line, I hover over the remaining line to equal the time it would take to fill out the remainder; before folding it out of my brother's view.

I need to force the folded slip into the reception box that is ready to over flow and clasp it shut with some force. Ahead is the beaten cemented path leading to the worn-down mansion still under conversion to the recreation center as promised. How it is practically devoid of any construction activity raises a level of skepticism. To my own lack of observation, there is clearly involvement differing from when it was a rotted dwelling, attributing to my traceur's admiration of architecture.

"Throwing that scroll in would be a better alternative." I suggest.

"That is what the education line is for." He refreshes the memory with a downward thrust of his beastly cat pad over my shoulder.

"Right." I confirm without him ever knowing that just my name and number are on that single wrinkled sheet.

To the extent we both wanted to be out in this final occasion of a night, we could not do anything less than accept the judgment of Trident's parents wanting us safe. They are two of the last mammals we know to even have offspring. Though one fact to take away from our acquired knowledge, is to make the best of what we have.

The prior day, we had purchased several delights of glucose and sodium to put us at ease of what we had triumphed over.

"You do realize," I somberly put out as I am flipping through our disk collection, "they are spoiling us on the cause that we are the finale of mammals."

"As optimistic as I we should be, you are not wrong." He forcibly comes to face the reality we have been born into. From behind the display panel, he pulls out the media cable and replaces it with a definite snap that is most stab to my ears.

"I made sure to thank them as always," to back up my discomfort. "Now with time free from the education, I am buying you a switcher so to get the full use of this set up."

"Your sire and dam would have done no different." He ignores my tech comment in a grip of the past I have advanced beyond. "Yet while on your topic of caring for a product's lifespan, you really don't want to eat while playing? We are the last, so why not go all out and risk a few grease-stained controllers?"

"Don't forcibly tempt me," I plead in resurgence of all desire to avoid external control that is not mine."

"These are MY controllers." the feline reclaims, "feel free to get them dirty."

"I will seek the opinions of Losse and Jasmine," I voice out the moment my ears pick up his mother unleashing the latch on the door and allowing in both the puma and lupine.

"Too close, both of you," she scolds, "I would rather the two of you stay put than be this late."

Though I agree with the adult, my optimistic persona gravitates that they are here, and safe.

"The crab ran goon!" their one son erupts from behind the display, once fitting in the multi colored cables."

"Right." I arise up my paws in recollection. Passing into the hall, I meet an adolescent female who will never be a matrilineal much to everyone's misfortune. Yet that will not change the love Trident has for her.

"Jasmine!" I introduce with a cock of my brow meeting my ear fold. The puma is bearing a rack of bottled beverages that are misty with chilled temperature. How they remained so in transporting here is not of my concern.

"Virgin, I assure you, Forjah." Folding back my pointed ears and eyes narrowed, I part lips and fight the newly induced discomfort with . . .

"I too am virgin." A scoff escapes from Losse, who is directly behind her and bringing a single lupine pad to her lips as Jasmine diverts her attention between her and me.

"Sheltered and genuine," my most trusted lupus details. Obviously, it is a form of a joke only understood between them. For I know how, "disrespectful" she can be among whom I know.

Moving past to join her male companion in the game room, I give Losse an embrace before she follows me into the galley where she assists me in retrieving the toasted tortillas and crustacean meat sauce.

Despite my overexposure and apathy combined, Losse gives a startled jump when the siren rings out from the exterior of the den.

"You two really did cut it close." I voice out in newfound concern. She bows her blackened head with sealed eyes.

"His mother stated we cannot take risks anymore; the last of us, she reassured." I too bow to the varg who is one that could never have a successor of any importance.

In an instant that perks our ears in equal astonishment, there is an individual yet familiar tone in the ring of the siren. Without warning, Losse grabs both the dip and the tortillas and points her nose with a directional point of her ears behind me.

Reversing my tail, I meet the outstretched bestial paw bearing an audio communicator. The mother cougar passes the device into my paw where I turn and make my way down hall to my best mates.

"Forjah?"

"You successfully pronounced my name," I negatively speak out in monotone, fighting the agitation of conversing through a line.

"My title is Clevarest." He initiates directly to a satisfying point. "I have come across your application this night."

My hinds halt at a snap of bipedal joints while a gulp escapes my maw.

"Ah, I detect your unexpected reaction. I am simply offering you a position here at Escape, if you so will it. Don't have concern for an interview. I would like to set that up with you at mid-day tomorrow."

My exhale pours forth like an anxious floodgate as I fall against the wall in loud beat of my shoulder blades. He instructs the combination to the main gate as an easy three digits before I finally let out "A name, number." I recall to the info I had listed only earlier today."

"Bare minimum indeed," he agrees before restating, "sun high tomorrow." The communicating terminates and I am left alone in the corridor interior where the primary sound is the start-up screen of Trident's 6th generation console.

Raising a paw to my aching head beating against the reinforced wall surface, I seal my eyes in emotions I cannot isolate from one another. All beastly instinct is sending off both negative and positive signals between my psyche and biology.

"Fox?" Losse interjects with my condensed name, in

obvious awareness of my withdrawn silence as I select my character in a dazed wide-eyed glare at the pixels of the past. Forcing my sight on her form settled in the body cushion, I give a slight yet noticeable head shake before questioning Trident.

"You claim none have been hired at Escape?"

"None," he ratifies with healthy portion of crustacean dip.

"Not even an opening date," Jasmine adds in unexpectedly. Returning eye site to Losse, she receives me again where I mouth a "No". Respect is with her for my state of mentality, which is at a minim point after finding this official. Yet I cannot help feeling so set off. How am I the first to be as much as contacted by this Clevarest? Why is a fear arising so similar to the one I have known since kit-hood when hearing those howls and roars in the night; that of those looking for blood . . .

Jasmine selects a stage, followed by the lengthy yet iconic loading screen as we each prepare for battle. Breaking into my sense is the black pelted paw of Losse inviting me to share the body pillow. I accept and join her with controller held out in the ready. Thankful I am, they are here at my side, for tomorrow is an unusual but accepted duration I must independently pursue.

SCENIC 2

There is factual evidence associating with my instinctual withdrawal into unresponsiveness. Every amount of focus extends out to the gate I have never seen open. For it remains closed as does my mind.

Jasmine, conveniently dragged us on her strive to claim the modern revision of Homeothermic Biology; despite the irony of our generation being the last.

"It may never need an update," I optimistically present, intent on diverting attention from my silence.

"With imposed rarity, now it may be at its cheapest point," Losse references to the future ahead. Like any exclusively produced item, the rarity increases over time along with the value held by each appraiser.

Trident stands aside Jasmine while she requests her pre-order and Losse makes her way to the new arrivals shelved at the storefront. I take my retreat behind the ever-stocked shelves absorbing the entirety of my form in bound spines. If I am to be abandoned to time without recorded document, so be a non-existent fate of an inkless dark age. I do eternally recall when inked symbols put me in direct tune with expertly crafted passages, forming a hypothetical context built into an expansive world. Yet, the joy of a text-based universe came to its traumatizing climax when I made the discovery of Chiroptera Quad, a series grabbing my heart at claw point by the second paragraph of page two, forming a connection directly to cognition and spirit. The protagonist is exactly who I wanted to perceive, with personality and actions taken at my approval and prediction. His survival drive is brought out by exposing every one of my emotions; even to the point I was driven to sickness of body and mind, as the writer employed. He took advantage of my body to read his work by inducing mentality through physicality, leading to an implanted sense of text-based malevolence, yet an implant of welcomed permanence. Chiroptera Quad is of the relatable level I previously defined as unattainable, proving it took a specified writer to spark this sensory untapped.

Now the story is more than literature. For it is a document making resided-rest in my memory bank, present even now. It leads influentially, without stray, assuredly on point. Comparing to my hinds forwarding through the overstocked shelves securely bolted to ensure the structural weight.

In the dead, clustered towers of worn and wrinkled spines, no title draws me nor does a spinal design entice. My acquired gain is isolation as the lone dog burdened with a shady first interview. A scheduled encounter set behind that corroded gateway, locked by three digits. Numbers are encountered throughout every wakening moment; yet those particular three granted only the previous night, are retained to my unlikable extent.

This trek is of identical familiarity, despite the overlaying sense, present only behind my optic nerves, tracking the steps in synch with memorizing the tri-combination. While Jasmine clutches the binding, chatter arises amongst her, Losse, and Trident on the exact subject of the activities beyond the stone enclosure. This wall lines the street side we have traveled since our legs could support us. None cared about the decaying mansion, expressed interest in the demesne, or even trespassed. Now I realize that none had a purpose to enter the property, making me the first to have a reason in the form of a request.

The distance between my three colleagues and me increases. My pace decreases before setting stance directly before the rusted gateway. I grant no alert to my companions upon grasping the first of the comb discs in orienting the worn lock.

Unintentional, yet expected, the rotations warn every ear in proximity. I too have never seen beyond these walls or witnessed the iron barrier opened. Am I changing that by the instigation of offered employment? Or am I a victim to a prank leading into humiliation?

"Forjah?" slips my name from the passive observation of Trident. One digit remains to correspond in approach of the outcome. A dividend conclusion tearing mentally with utmost uncertainty. I have done miraculously to manage survival for my existing duration as a member of the refining era. Risk has been present as to which I have declined or accepted under which of the two opts as the best fit. Now offers a risk, set behind a metallic combination lock. One turn for the risk of my choosing in proceeding.

A satisfied sound seizes the moment from me and releases a chatter of hushes from the surrounding street. Yet as a traceur, I have learned to ignore stares. For it is the metallic clink distinguished by the clank of detaching gears. Yet the alternative glee transitions through my auditory sensors the moment the corroded bars withdraws inward, allowing for entry.

"An interview has my calling." My maw musters to my sight veering down over the pavement I have stepped beyond, returning the gate to locked position. I have no additional input nor is my being accepting this in mind.

Trident is gleeful for my opportunity, following the app from earlier, though my three companions are in full right to worry despite the thrill arising over sense of consciousness. I am in a position most desired by all gawking from the asphalt intersection. The deep prolonged anticipation of witnessing one enter into the grounds would theoretically prove exemplary; yet why am I that candidate? Daring not to glare back, there may be a mob of onlookers made of proximate bystanders. The one fact residing with me is my employment progression toward Escape's grand opening.

Archaic in design lost to time, every corroded bolt with faded fragmenting stone serves eras proceeding my birth, before gargoyles came into existence. The urban decay is most unwelcoming, to an extent similar to ruins corrupted by eternal wanderers of the supernatural.
Leading up to the cold grasp, I latch over the handles. Sound from the interior reaches my ears to a recognizable degree, and making entry confirms these auditory receptors.

Forcing the hinged planks outward, I enter and close myself from the outsiders. Before me is the belly of the rundown lodge. Tarps and steel scaffoldings are positioned in every corner supporting rugged garbed crafters scraping away dried paint and replacing every rotted plank. Not one takes notice, extending upon rumor that only "those accepted" enter Escape.
Theoretically, I belong here with utmost right.

Beneath the overhang of the second level balcony, I have selected the opened rear door as my destination. It may lead to the commander yet will assuredly provide an extensive view of the event grounds.

Only my eye and paw make it in motion before an approaching figure catches sight of me en route. I have a limited amount of instance to even identify the creature before he calls out.

"Forjah," greets the now identified mangut. Yet it is not my outspoken title that is blindsiding me. It is the two names I have long abandoned.

"The offspring," he figures in recertification. "How I have desired the pleasure of encountering the descendent of my dear ally." Though it may be a form of politeness to extend the intro, he uncoordinatedly knows more than I do of him.

"Commander Clevarest is my title. I have striven to surface this site out of ruin and into a lively recreation. Now I am seeking to employ a tactical crew." Directing out from the roar of tools and into a corridor, he leads into a sort of study with an enlarged window pane overlooking the external grounds. Aside the commander, I take in the concrete pouring in strategically arranged sections, outlining a track layout.

"Batting, discus, and especially go karts are the primary operations. The duration of shifts is scheduled from light to dusk by avoiding the predation of night. Yet it will thrive in the light granted."

"Most productive," I comment with little remaining to define in reaction. With that vague observational output, Clevarest offers a seat with furthering institution of the interview process. Yet he admits to an explanation most confounding in a sense of applying for employment.

"My hiring and need for a crew expand beyond seeking those qualified. Your sire and I coexisted within an alliance," the canid reveals to my reawakened awe. "His mate became your dame, bearing her first and last. By a visual inherit, your facials are reminiscent of her rather than him. Knowing after the conclusion of the refining generation that I wanted to employ within peers, my mind sought to locate the son of my friend."

Repositioning into a relaxed position, I am finding my mind attempting to solve his meaning. He was looking for me from the first moment of advertising? I had not applied before Trident's motivation, yet this is what Clevarest awaited?

"I strategized that in offering a high salary, everyone would apply, including you. By reducing the time it would take to locate, the exploit proved accomplishing."

His statement has reduced my bodily activity to a low pulse barely managing a throb. He orchestrated this scheme to specifically locate one dog: every overlooked app, just a step before my own turned up?

"If the influence my colleague has raised you in proves as respectful and devoted as he, I am at full approval of bringing you on board." In a collective acquire of emotional empowered contemplation, he finalizes with. "You are accepted as long as you accept the position, Forjah. In substitution of chatting to prove your worth, accept this job offer and physically prove you are capable and worthy to retain it."

As an individual with a personality unmatched, I have the full amount of respect of his ploy to acquire the right crew. He wants action and not account. This is the opportunity coveted, obstructed by my opt in obligation. Yet in this perspective, such a specified position is a fit for a deviated dog. Introspectively, this is not about my desires; it is about my morally personified accommodations.

"I welcome your offer," I finalized.

Long into the building and furnishing of the ancient settlement, I humbly request to Clevarest for an outdoor position. I am not against grounds keeping, as it would be a peaceful and isolated duty. Though, every expectation numbs my naive mind when he assigns me to go kart operating, despite my lack of understanding how a basic machine functions. Though this is only a surface job as he describes, I do recommend one who can maintain the engine internals. Thus, Trident is hired as mechanic for his devotion to machinery. To think this all stemmed from his curiosity as a kit for how complex systems worked.

"Modified mower engine," the cougar identifies. "Hygiene against the grease will be the first and prolonged obstacle."

"Don't embrace Jasmine with blackened paws," I suggest, "or lip smack her with petroleum breath."

Secondary, he and I are informed that public love of a charming feminine is to greet at the lodge entrance. After much discussion on the needs of the business and what they can offer, both Jasmine and Losse are brought on board upon proving their worth.

With one last update before we prepared for the grand opening, Trident approaches our commander with suggestion of a new hire. The individual he refers to is beyond my relationship zone; yet upon the dog's stare is admiration for the cougar's input. Only days later, a new recruit arrives on the track; Ares, a spherical-eyed crocuta of wise glare and respectful persona. Knowing the robust nature of hagines, the physical prowess is most admirable. Primarily, Trident will devote to maintenance while Ares and I focus on the track.

With employed training documented in our minds and with the familiarity at paw tips, the three of us look onward to the gate, ready to allow entry to the anticipated crowd. Losse and Jasmine are register ready with their best discipline glare of forcing positive attitudes in representation of Escape. With engines primed and burning for this recreational birth, they will assuredly keep hot until the cool down of nocturnal light.

Cleverast approaches the entrance path with key-ring in paw, holding them up in announcement of this grand moment. The lock will click, hinges will creek, and engines will accelerate.

The glee to be gained here from bat smashers to tire skids will occur under our watchful eye; the eye of the escapists.

SCENIC 3

The improvements in the engines are quite noticeable in our upgraded go karts.

"Trident," I call over, "these acceleration upgrades are exquisite!"

"Delighted you agree" the puma sends over. "To tell you the truth I was afraid about breaking in these new systems. So thanks for being the crash dummies."

"We all must take life-threatening risks."

"Drivers will finally know the true adrenaline impulse," Ares outburst with an engine sputter. I know what he means; kits always are granted a thrill here on the track. But it is the adults who want fun to an extreme. Now we have our answer with these additional sprint carts.

Now is the time to put the advancement to the extreme.

"Let us off the track; these wheels need some off-roading." After the hagine and I complete one lap, Trident has the gate beam pulled away to release us. I lead the way onto Escape's walking paths. Approaching up ahead perches a park bench, providing an obstacle I welcome. I define, with my instinct of timing, the path just right, gradually increasing speed by drawing the grip bars back, matching what should be the required speed to add in a drift. My careful adaptation proves effective once again as I curve around the wooden seat like a masse shot. Just ahead, Ares intersects my path, immediately breaking through our entry gateway with lack of traction.

"Always leave room for improvement!" He communicates over to Trident.

"Really? What ideas do you have?"

"I'll pass on a list," he confides.

Ares decides to take our new karts to levels only he would attempt, but I need a break from the cockpit and decide to head back in. Rounding the north side of our station, I maneuver into the kart lane where the rest are positioned.

Back upon the concrete platform, I bring my body into a great spinal and limb stretch.

The surface is quite cold beneath my forepaws after the heat of the engine. Here in the Escape lodge, all is just as quiet as the skies above.

"I wish we could all learn from Ares," Trident tells Jasmine and me. "He learns so fast, there are none who can keep up with him."

"Agreed," ratifies the female cougar. "To have him on our side is a blessing."

Our side? Whatever could she mean and why would Ares ever be against us? Commenting on this newly arisen thought is the proper action, but I choose not to. Something insignificant as a choice of linguistics is rarely a meaningful event. Never will it serve a deep purpose. "I feel like we are all on a different level. None of us are ever equal."

"We follow you, Fox. You brought us in union and keep us together. You are our link that lead us to employment."

All I did was pass the message between them and Clevarest. If misunderstanding their independence proves true, they need to learn to function without me. I know that day will come as equally as they do not. Departing, I make my way to the vault in need of gathering my gear and deviate some time to myself.

I need some escape in order to refresh my mind and vitality. But the fact drowned deeply within me is of past purpose and continuous depression. A feeling that comes and has yet to depart from now. It is why I desire solitude while silently excusing myself from the track, leaving the cougars to observe the new go kart's capability.

Inputting my lock combo, I open the steel door that still bears the name marquee that always acts in dreadful recall. It is an inheritance that was automatically passed on to me after employment. My sire left me zilch. His concentrated life exists outside my ignorance as well as my inquiry.

Deciding that the offspring silently stand before the locker of a dog is odd to anyone that may come in. I begin removing my operator uniform and change into my traceur's garb. To the approval of isolation, I am alone here in the vault hoard. Placing myself upon the pine polished bench, I force myself to let this depressing sorrowful moment pass.

I flex my legs so my knees meet my chest and then layer my forearms with my muzzles' underside atop.

I so desire to move on from what proves so difficult to let go of. Nothing is holding me here. Escape can do just fine without me. But until my passing comes, I need to forward on until its finale arrival.

This room is as empty as I feel, hollow, with much lost

over time.   Even the open unoccupied lockers reflect my insignificance and worthlessness. From their rusted cold ware to the bland concrete backdrops . . .

"Concrete?"   I voice in a hushed growl echoing in the

INFERTILE CONCEPTION

In this reality, all mammals have become infertile for an unknown cause our cure.
At the birth of the final generation, the humble yet wise reptilian race concocted a solution for their warmblooded allies.

empty quarters.   Looking down the line of opened doors and through the vents of those claimed, it is revealed in my eye that everyone has a concrete rear matching the stone walls. All but one . . .

Returning to my own, I find the red steel back drop I have always known. But why is its construction different? Removing my uniform and flight suit from their hooks, I set them on the bench to allow a clear view of the polished metal inward wall. At my paws touch, it is crimson thick steel far from the likeness of the thin rusted metal that actual lockers are made of. For a more detailed test, I ball a paw into a fist and thrust it upon the metal

surface. The points of my ears rise to an auditory most hollow . .
.

Immediately, I begin emptying out the entirety by placing my gear carelessly upon the bench. Then I begin running both digits and eyesight in focus over the surface to feel for any newly suspicious sign, starting from the bottom and working my way up. Other than the hook-holds, I find one factor standing out among the rest. A single screw positioned at the top right corner on the underside of the locker roof. I have noticed it in the past but never gave it a second thought. However, I am noticing that it is the one screw with no visible signs of equal construction.

Pushing and pulling upon it does nothing, but maybe I should use it as is meant to function. Taking the head between my pointer and thumb claw, I turn it clockwise to find it loose and rotatable. Just a millimeter away from the surface, my keen ears detect what sounds like cogs and gears sounding just behind the steel locker wall. With a machine-like heave, the red backdrop drops down on a pair of slides to completely retract into the floor; revealing a hidden cargo area beyond. Immediately, a familiar remaining musk comes over me and recalls the times long expired.

I attempt hold back the paralysis the scent brings back to me with a somewhat unwelcome return. No one before or since has entered this space, for the identification of his remainder had all but vanished when I took over.

Retrieving the hidden gear, I find various items I do not recognize. An alternative uniform suit of slate gray and comparative green with an ID tag, a torso armor piece, a helmet of the similar make, and flexible grip-gloves proportionally manufactured for a dog's paws. Yet my memory is quenched upon the last item retrieved from a rack above. A set of metallic-framed goggles.

Memory floods my mind in an unrepressed recall recaptured. He bore these to the synonymous extent of identity.

I never gave this eyewear a detailed theory, but now having found that he left them inside a hidden cache within his locker, it presents as most peculiar.

When the creaking hinges of the door sound from across the room, I am slightly brought out of all conspiring thought. Quickly and swiftly returning the gear into the hidden cargo, my vulpine instinct clandestinely impulses the return to concealment. What remains of the findings are the slightly rusted goggles in the pad of my dominant paw as a comforting reminder of my past duration.

Attempting to inverse the screw proves no use, but when I simply pull from the top, the concealed machines reactivate and bring the wall back up and the screw returns to its retracted position.

"Cleverly designed," I comment.

Once securing my own personal gear back into the locker, I harness the pack over my shoulder, lock the door, and slip the goggles over my ears. Padding bare-pawed over the carpet, they will soon be feeling the planks beneath them, then the concrete molding, succeeded by the grass-cut earth, only to return upon carpet before nightfall. Rounding the corner of the central enclosure, two individuals have entered and are coming my way. I give no attention as we are about to pass, in favor of time to myself to escape into my own persona.

"DOG!" one of them gasps, with a grunt followed by the other in my direction. Just as I am passing a glance over, the dog, the male lorinae, thrusts his paw into my chest, clamping my shirt and pulling me back behind the cover of the locker line.

"THERE IS NO WEARING THOSE HERE!" he scowls with disgust, thrashing the goggles from my head and insisting I hide them beneath my torso garment.

"A master should strive cautionary." the female, a barramys, advises. The primate looks between us and lets out a heated breath, ". . . right." The entry door again opens and they push me toward the further of the room. "Lead on master. The secluded passage is the primary target."

I give no response, in absolute misunderstanding. But my impulse is the thrusting of his foot against my back, "Move your tail!" he hastily forces. I move in silence, but pick up my pace when they both begin to silently patter at my side.

"Sprint ahead to prepare the passage." The marsupial does as he requests by taking off on gentle patters of her delicate toes. As a traceur, I highly admire a quiet paw. We, too, pick up our pace and the only paws I can hear are our own. Rounding the final row of lockers, I find her entering in a code upon a locker with speed and has it open in only a brief moment. It is completely empty but bares the same red steal back as does mine.

"Another? What could this one hide?" Instead of rotating a screw, the rodent-like beast clenches her paw upon a wall hook, turning it in a few directions in a way similar to a rotary lock. We hear an identical sound of mechanical wiring and it too falls to the floor; revealing a dark passage.

The lorinae peers over the blocking locker wall before signaling, "Clear!" His companion then motions her tail into the locker by requesting, "After you, master." I part my lips in a droop, but no verbals pass off my tongue. I am in absolute shock of what I do not know is happening, but my instinct is acting as primer for a nicely kindled fire in my senses.

Moving forward before the open door, I clutch the goggles while placing my first paw over the locker and into the stone carved mouth. The draft of the deep earth is extreme, but my fur counteracts it with a fluff up on my nape. My irises dilate to let in the light they have absorbed throughout the day and I can see the tunnel is deep and long with just a fraction of light toward its bending trail. She comes in behind me, followed by her partner, who pulls the locker door closed as it automatically locks itself. Just as he is readying to pull the secret door closed, figures behind the vent holes pass by with loud cheers of a successful work day. Once they are safely out of sight, the canid pulls the door up to shut and secure it again. Upon its closure, I see a particular nob that is obviously on the opposite side of the hanger, serving as a way back in.

"Delve in," he announces. I have no idea who these two are or where I am leading despite my paws clenching tightly to the goggles in reassurance, combatting any amount of fear.

SCENIC 4

The same golden light I picked up before, in the tunnel beginning, has grown immensely strong as we approach the source. Moments after making our way down the passage, voices begin dancing their melodic echoes down the tube like a massive brass kin instrument. They are voices of various maturity and of both genders, yet the one likeness they all share is common joy of intense, positive vitality.

My ears have not received such charisma in a great while. So long, it seems foreign; but I am possibly thinking in a blinded way. Many have come to pass, providing a newfound celebratory reason. The grief of mourning is so far developed and impacting, that I have given little attention of focus or recognition to recollect times of fondness. My pain has always been a shield without withdrawal, preventing the finding of a solace. Why now am I being touched for the first time in so long; why are these cheerful chimes touching me like none before?

My two guides break through the final entrance and leave me to enter on my own. The stone is giving way to soft earth where my paws move forward onto the dark soil. I am presented with multiple glares of various glittering locations, shimmering in all directions, in what appears to be a large underground grotto.

Only upon my eyes reverse dilating, do I begin adjusting to exactly what I've stumbled upon. Before me is a great growth of a tree root wider than an aircraft carrier's belly. Hollowed out on its surface stretches a carved trail lined with individual shelters, ascending the trunk to the point of a darkened cave mouth. The light sources emitting from these enclosures are artificial with no external light emitting anywhere above. Fumes emit from fires and other production sources, escaping into vents clearly visible in the earth ceiling. Obviously, this development was established long before my time.

Wherever my location is, every point of instinct halts any further approach. Upon sighting an occupant wearing similar goggles to those I instructively influenced, the best option impulses in the form of reapplying to position upon my scalp by wrapping under my ears. To experience the form of his cranial curve is a limited comparison as my own is sharpened differently, having limited resemblance to him both visually and personified. Though at this point of comfortably fitting the strapped eyewear over my ears, the image of the original owner comes into view. It is distantly and clearly visible amongst the dwellers of this cave.

Through the passing individuals perches his image, framed in a misshapen boarder. Hurriedly maneuvering in direct path of the image to a freedom and isolation as the vulpine like to be, I ascend upon the plank boardwalk to descend to my knees before the mounds of wilted efflorescence. A memorial. Why here, among a mural of roughly framed images of both mammal and reptile. What is it he shares with these depicted individuals apart from an obvious loss of life?

The relief I received in the arrival is all but dying as the darkness blooms here. The pain is to an ever expanding extreme where I suffer on in the ponder of why to remain.

"Our colleague's passing brings out more than moist ducts," an elevated palpitates.

"I have never stopped," I reply by bringing eyes out of my paw to meet the voice holder. In the moment of locking eye

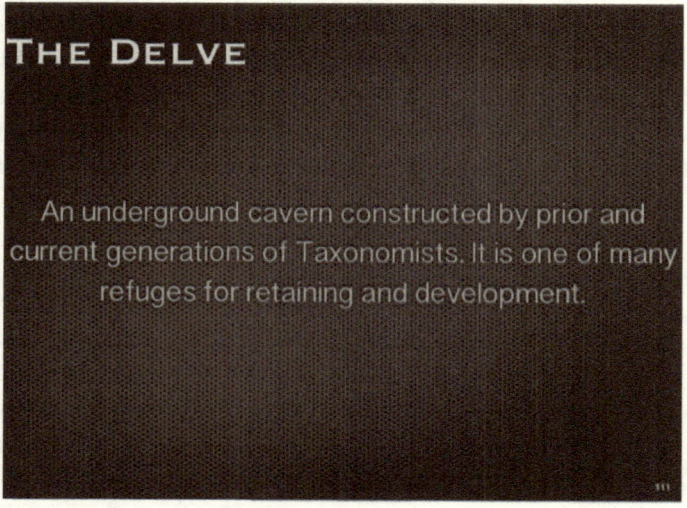

THE DELVE

An underground cavern constructed by prior and current generations of Taxonomists. It is one of many refuges for retaining and development.

contact does his expression turn horrific with paw moving to a protruding rod from behind his shoulder. Sliding it up and over, it reveals a pointed blade zeroing in my direction.

"You are not taxonomist nor candidate." The dingo raises his muzzle in howls of environmental distress, carrying through without need for a mass warning transmission. Many retreat while responders heed to my announced intrude. I focus in at the threat of advanced steel, but the blindsiding extremity prevents any retrieval of my own tool of defense secured at belt strap.

My ears pick up the familiar and definite sound of steel unsheathed, along with the withdraws of tools beyond sensory recognition. I have no further desire to live. If I am to be taken down here and now, the pain will only be lasting a bit longer in duration.

Realigning my miss-inherited eyetot the image of my paternal beginning and into his formal posed-eyes, one last time, I voice out, ". . . sweet sleep, please bid me."

I settle folded paws over my thighs and lay my tail flat out and raise up my muzzle to the roof with closed eyes to await my passing. My last breath is the entirety of my mental concentration. But no matter how much I want to divert my sense into nothing, I cannot shake the sounds of approaching paws kicking up dirt before clamoring over the wooden planks. My fear is great and my pulse furiously runs, my temp escalates into inferno. Tears again are escaping my eyes, but I force my will to cling as my spirit leaves and is welcomed by the afterlife.

"To whom is the intruding dog?" demands a voice directly overhead. I make no response and continue to pant out in uncontrollable breaths.

"Lower all tools at our defense. He has not made any assault. Therefore, we will treat him with equal response." The order brings my eyes shot open and returns to the reality I have always known. Before me is a corsac of light crop brown dressed in a silver flowing garb and black leather belt. He turns to his side and I determine by the action of his tail that he is showing peace.

"We are not in great need of who you are. But we must know how you came into our dwelling." Anyone knows that honesty is the right answer in this time, here and now.

"I found a hidden space behind my sire's locker in the Escape vault. It was garments I do not recognize and this pair of goggles that I remember him bearing. When I put them on, two individuals lead in upon, scolding me for bearing them outside. Having no idea what they meant, I followed without question in response to my curiosity."

The dog calls out the names of my transport, beckoning them near. When they arrive, they glance at me with paws resting on the roots of their tails and muzzles at the ground.

The lorinea steps in front of his partner and takes full credit for the mistake. "I am sorry, Dixon. I assumed he was a Taxonomist by the goggle make." The corsac dog bows and thanks them both, which surprises the couple, who each let out a reassuring breath. Coming back to my attention, Dixon, as his name is revealed to be, projects out.

"If you do not wish to reveal your name, then we will be forced to transport you back to the surface and seal off the passage you came through." After approving my request to stand, I return to my paws and voice out.

"That is at my full approval." This triggers many huffs from every direction of the inhabitance.

"Most unexpected,.." the barramys observes with an awkward directional glare. "Can't define you as comparable to anyone," she then adds in. The blindsided admiration is a definite sign to my lack of precaution and willingness of submission in territory not my own, where I have willfully trespassed. Moral code indeed, paired with my need for an end.

"I will respect your . . . privacy," I decide to define it as with a raise of my pointer claw to the framed image, "but why are you still mourning him amongst others? My sire's passing came long before."

The next happening is a sound burst of objections, scoffs, and dilated pupils.

"SIRE?" roars a feline from the crowd.

I have made a complete circle of the surrounding individuals and come right back to Dixon, giving him a look for a needed answer.

"Are you as you claim?" the vulpes corsac prays out.

I flare up ears at his response. "Of course! His mate is my dam. When two are in love, it outcomes to a biological result of the two." Now directing my pointer claws back upon myself, I restate.

"I am of the refining generation; the last of mammals. I am their one and only offspring."

"Your Goggles," Dixon accordingly requires. Folding my ears, I remove them and transfer into his paws. He gives an internal inspection, ultimately coming to hold them at his breast before confidently alarming to all around.

"This set is genuine to our ally." Apart from my ignorance to a number of protests, many remain quiet at the declaration. Dixon then pulls me forward and away from the faded images mounted above warmth-deprived petals. He expands his paws outward to his fellow companions addressing . . .

"My allies, comrades, friends. There is not an individual alive who mourns a fallen companion extensively greater than their own kin. Let us welcome this finale purist into the reality long established." Upon request of my moniker, I reveal it without any amount of withholding.

"Let us welcome Forjah, as our guest," he promises while palming the goggles. "Forjah, I would be obliged in returning these to you. But you are not yet qualified."

"Qualified?"

Before descending the steps, he makes one last turn and sincerely holds my concentrated focus.

"You Fox, have only the title of Taxonomist memorized."

Like the intro to a historically chocked-full documentary, the info Dixon feeds into my mind details that I am the direct offspring of a delver in Taxonomy, specifically dealing with tactical defense of oneself and wholesome kin. With a common enemy, I can only gravitate to gargoyles. It is here in the Delve, he describes as the grounds for offensive and defensive.

"Taxons are a field in counteraction to the reptile\mammal hybrids? I am tempted to inquire why you hide away from more than gargoyles?"

Upon presenting taxon as a range of individual conducts, he holds back in vague detail of . . .

"You only know your reality, Forjah. You do not fathom the architecture behind its visuals or imagine beyond its perception. When you feel you are set to take it in, return here for instruction."

Satisfaction is with me in every conceivable amount as Dixon sends for a chauffeur on foot. The fact I am not welcome here expands far beyond my desire for retained isolation. Bidding farewell, he appoints the escort to lead on in return to the surface. When it is clear, I open the false wall and step out, closing the door behind my guide. Thanking her before closing all connection to Taxonomy.

SCENIC 5

I do not immediately depart. Instead I return to the locker. Reapplying the screw, the wall again retracts and reveals the uniform of silver and green. I move it aside and reveal yet another passage to the skulk I want absolutely nothing to do with. Returning the wall into its closed position, I take my departure.

Today I am not bothering with a mobile transport, as I just need a strolling hike to incubate the accumulating thoughts. My paws pass from tiled flooring, onto heated asphalt, then over the rugged concrete roadside.

"A taxonomic origin." This is all I am dwelling over in what slips past my muzzle. They are not the most comforting impulses leading by instinct into the overshadowing trees, who are welcoming my comforting return to rural greenery.

The domestic life secluded me away for far too long, refraining on the cause it brings back memories of a longingly repressed past. To psyche exclusive knowledge, the accumulation of my origin remains here outside the concrete jungle. The reason for not returning is the pain of remembering the past long lost.

He selected my upbringing for the wild with safety paired

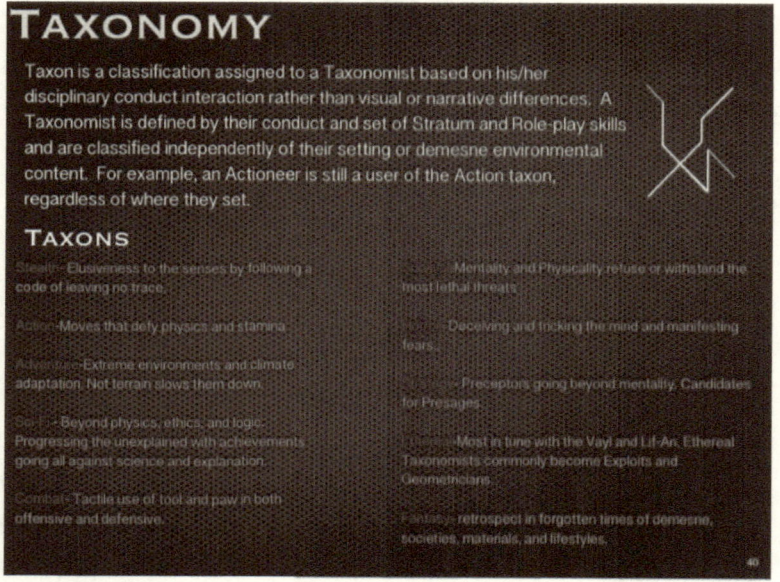

TAXONOMY

Taxon is a classification assigned to a Taxonomist based on his/her disciplinary conduct interaction rather than visual or narrative differences. A Taxonomist is defined by their conduct and set of Stratum and Role-play skills and are classified independently of their setting or demesne environmental content. For example, an Actioneer is still a user of the Action taxon, regardless of where they set.

TAXONS

Stealth- Elusiveness to the senses by following a code of leaving no trace.

Action-Moves that defy physics and stamina.

Adventure-Extreme environments and climate adaptation. Not terrain slows them down.

Sci-Fi - Beyond physics, ethics, and logic. Progressing the unexplained with achievements going all against science and explanation.

Combat- Tactile use of tool and paw in both offensive and defensive.

Horror- Mentality and Physicality refuse or withstand the most lethal threats.

Thriller- Deceiving and tricking the mind and manifesting fears.

Mystery- Preceptors going beyond mentality. Candidates for Presages.

Fiction-Most in tune with the Vayl and Lif-An. Ethereal Taxonomists commonly become Exploits and Geometricians.

Fantasy- retrospect in forgotten times of demesne, societies, materials, and lifestyles.

40

against the unexpected enemy. He spent a great longevity of time, even before my conception. A dugout disguised to a point as unrecognizable to my dog body, prior to molting the dark fur of my whelp-hood. My intention was never to realign an approach, but my paws forward their momentum to the precise destination. As a kit, I did not want change, but my biological growth altered my desires. Being vulpine, my adaptation is high, rendering nothing out of my retainment capability.

Tall grass grows furtively in over the path of my immature days. But the rout is as familiar to my immensely sized paws as when they were undeveloped. Trees tower and remain untouched, every flower seasonally returning to bloom, the lone aery still mounted on location. The one significant change, is the returning vulpine; who is now a dog.

The first I see are those familiar oaken branches I climbed prior to becoming a traceur. Upon discovery of the newly gained sense, I wanted to be engulfed in the branches. In the moment of prohibited climbing, I literally made it my territory.

Passing over hill with tips of ears raised, I overstep the rise and see it for the first time with an adult's perspective. Its shimmering green are signs of welcoming back the last of the kin, who is feeling a charge of confidence shadowing the grief. When before its trunk, I collapse upon as if embracing a rescued friend; inhaling the wood scent and massaging paw pads over its bark. All this time, I thought returning here would only devastate me in emotional loss. But here I am renewed with unattainable joy counteracting all doubt.

"Is it superior to be close to my past rather than keeping away?" Spaced between the tree roots and the cliff wall is a root grown mass forming a tangled weaving. Prying it from the ground reveals the dark tunnel entrance to my birth den. Perceiving beyond mental incubation, I go headfirst in allowing the tunnel passage to engulf me in its cold earthy mouth. The walls hug against my robust dog form in geological acceptance as the accommodated species. Constructively dug only for vulpine at a level impassible by gargoyle. Strategically clandestine for concealment outside the ignorance of enemy and even ally.

His partner informed that he courted her exclusively. Against the last of the male vulpes chemical ardor, the suitor refrained from him in her own chemically charged reluctance. Yet that dog's own passion for my maternal vixen drove him to hastily carve this den. How this materialistic shelter altered her perspective of him is beyond my fathoming. The negative impulse she initiated against "his burn for her" aroused him to provide a quarters of her appeasing?

"The ultimatum result of their courtship is myself." I am fortunate not only to be the exclusive offspring, but an infertile member of the refining generation. Thankful not being victim to biological chemicals beyond control.

The inclining shaft is no match for my fully adapted night vision. The opposing mouth comes into view before I nose kiss the cool surface of the steel trapdoor. It opens on the creak of

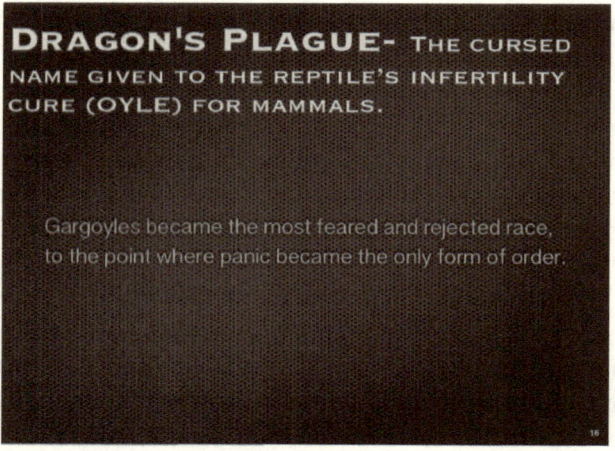

DRAGON'S PLAGUE- THE CURSED NAME GIVEN TO THE REPTILE'S INFERTILITY CURE (OYLE) FOR MAMMALS.

Gargoyles became the most feared and rejected race, to the point where panic became the only form of order.

corroded hinges while I enter into the darkness of the den. Crawling out with eyes closed intently on preparing for the moment, I free the door from grip and it seals firmly behind.

The whole interior, an entrapment of cold with the most limited heat withheld. Now is the time to return my vision to the dwelling I once knew and familiarize with newfound perspective.

Pulling back my lids, my night vision scents in the dark surroundings with the only light source being overhead. Everything, I mean everything is in place unchanged from time. Aside the skylight is the long stove pipe stretching down to the root of an iron stove. Where I huddled in the cold season awaiting my first ever solid meals.

There is a cruise layout the two shared while I always used the cushion bag. There it sits exactly where I abandoned with same impression my kit body made. Kneeling, I run my adult sized paw over the impression left on that final day. The feel of my original size connects me, as I never anticipated nor readily prepared. It is left completely unaffected while I have effectively achieved growth through survival.

Now my eyes track the familiar gaze to an impression in the stone I know better than anyone. A sort of tunnel mouth my paws could not keep from eroding down like the ever growing incisors of a rodentia. Neither she nor her mate thought I would make it far, but like my wild ancestors; I had created a nook in the earth enough for my kit body to claim as territory. I was motivated to cease the digging to retain my claw points, and did so only when they needed to rejuvenate more keratin to continue.

Collapsing upon my knees into the dug impression, I run my adult paws through the familiar soil and palm it by inhaling the earth scent of my kit hood. It is as though it represents my kin, reduced to geological soil. I, the last airing bloodline, feeling what is left of his kin and loved ones. Alone with limited past to recall nor future to forward into. My classification: dead-end with no continuation.

Warning was stated that an overthinking mind can be dangerous, to the extent of delusional insanity. Is this where I am now, breaking away from being sane and becoming loco? The more energy my mind claims, the greater the exhaustion fatigues my form. Curling up into the hole made by my kit paws, I let the darkness put me to slumber as I never thought it would.

SCENIC 6

"Full exertion!" Demands the familiar voice in the psyche recalling that first groundbreaking day. My paws, shins, and thighs ace to an exhausted extent. Sinuses burn at my heaving cardiovascular.

"Passion pushes beyond the limit of your physicality." Again rings the ever echoing voice. "Use your body and overpower what only your mind thinks your physicality is capable of." I press on over concrete with callused pads building frictional momentum. Finally, I take off in a dive. Landing the table top with fore's outstretched, I flex at elbow joints to carry the point of hind tips to tail tip in performance of the dive kong.

Pain now burns both in sinuses and abdominals, but it is nothing compared to this sensation of overpowering accomplishment. Without a care of those surrounding or embarrassment, I raise nose and forepaws to the air along with my bush tail. Pulling in a welcoming inhale.

Yes, I have now completed the dive kong for a time's first. But even more incredible is how much of a burst this developed from. Tracing is not a physical high alone, but a pairing with the wealth of my psyche. No sport is comparable to the art of displacement.

Stopping directly in front of my favored cool down location, I begin stretching to muscular satisfaction with assurance to appear genuinely domestic; as there exists irony in a wild dog preferring the urban structures as a practitioner. If only this accomplishment could be shared among fellow teammates; yet as the sport is exclusive, so am I in the discipline.

Proceeding through the glass door, the opposing handle taps the glass with a diminutive ring. Still, the need of a stopper remains despite the neglect.

Approaching the counter, I find a new set of facials before the register. A ratufa, sporting a pink tinted brow paired with corresponding ear points.

"Protein smoothy," I request. "Mixed berry, is my desire."

"You an athlete?" she mocks.

"Health is prioritized." I comment. She smirks in either an expression of smite or insulting tease.

"Limited assistance to pure mammals." She indirectly insults.

"Not near to the extent of our forefathers." I even out the conversation with positioned paws above my tail root awaiting her confirmation. When the order is placed, I proceed before the glass separating the wilderness park outside. I look forward to the autumn colors instituting their arrival, but now I just want to take in the last of current season's blooming blossoms. Even after that, what will tracing in the snow feel like?

"Hey dog." Comes the same stern voice of the rodent, placing the fruit concoction before me. The paws gripping the glass flex right in place where my prints will soon grip it.

"Appreciated." I extend. "I await its rejuvenating nutrients."

"Not with your lack of testosterone." With this finalizing insult, she turns her tail and begins clearing an additional table. Ignoring both the scar and thought she has placed in my mentality, I bring the rim of the glass to my lips and practically chug the iced fruit liquid; finding it quite sour compared to what I am used to. But with autumn blowing in and warmth dying away, I know the taste of freshened fruit will become absent until the prime of the succeeding thermal season.

After consuming the drink fully, I slurp the sides by my tongue to make the cleaning job easier and to ingest every amount. Placing it together on the wooded table plank and wiping my muzzle, I rise, return the stool, and proceed into the on-setting nightfall.

When the dorm door opens, it does not reduce any amount of being lost in the comic pages. Trident steps in surprised to see me baring the worn gloss print. I decide against moral judgment to not relate beyond my achievement of today's dive vault.

"Those survived?" He projects in extreme awe, "these are a beloved time's recall." Proclaiming while taking volume XLVII into his paws. Flipping through the page's memories, he is familiar with the digitized sheets to a great extent.

"I love new games." I comment by bringing up, "but retro is the birth of interactive digital revolution."

"Agreed." The cougar purrs while snatching up a volume I know well; LVI. "Volume LVI, page LXVI." Your mate's portrait." He transfers the open comic into my own paws retrospectively. "The story cut short," Trident details, "she may still be a bachelorette."

He suggestively refers to the love interest in my most

beloved comic series. The popularity has remained limited, favored mostly by the exclusion of my part in the last generation. When further progressing into the remainder of its run, I learned of the sacrifices of the protagonist. Disclosed not by his own admittance, but of the companions who counteracted his pure instinctual reliance. But with a new arrival unwillingly making the team, she and the lead were drawn to each other like neither had ever experienced. The enemy antagonist enraged him by depriving the sophisticate whelp; leaving him to solely develop not through influence, but instinct. He advanced into a domestic mutt with minimal morale yet a sense of who was truly a foe. Not being drawn to each other; the factor that did bring the dog and vixen to a leveling point was the conduct of their survival in a reality atrophied of natural selection. Only through time, did their chemicals alter the contact they shared.

"She is of the most absolute beauty." Which I know glamour upon with irises of an adult vulpine.

"You can totally match up to him. He may be skilled in militia exclusively, but you could give the same love he grants to her." This is why Trident is a cougar who will always be my close allied brother. No matter the depth of the vexation, he is always bright and ready to haul out of the deep pit.

"There is admiration building for your optimism," I describe," exiled from our birthing realm is secondary to your positivity."

"Don't limit it just to my own. A dog needs a strong sense as much as a tom."

Going into living in prosperity, I forcefully intervene with, "There is no longer a point." I exhale in reject. "We are the last mammal generation, the end in line with no chance for prosperity. Even the reptiles have failed attempting at healing our fertility. It is over Trident, once our refining era dies."

Am I really meaning these verbals passing my lips? Why is my spirit so unsure of my mind's process right now? Something in my body creating a numbing feeling all throughout to nose, tail, and limb. Yes, I never think correctly when ill. Now I know I am sick.

Sitting up and returning focus the cougar, his glare holds the same lost expression he received from my revelation. Yet, he worsens as I pull my trembling form up.

"Fox, what is ailing you?"

"Unsure," I relate with uncertainty, "I am sorry, my mind is not thinking clearly right now."

"Then you need rest." He recommends. As beneficial as it may be, my true desire proves to be the exact opposite. I am too restless and trembling with energy to convalesce. As peculiar as this presents, I give no questions as my instinctive desire for muscular motion cuts in and rejects any inquiry.

As though a departure for a long trek, Trident hugs me like an oversized constricting python. Padding a shoulder with his paw pad, he bids and advises.

"Heal up bro. The track will miss you for the duration; all its steel and cement." He departs behind the seal of the dorm door; where the tract bolt collides against the frame in synch with my traceur's paws furtively impacting the planks below my hammock.

Upon the audit mark of Trident's brute sized pads reaching ground level, I slip to the iron barricaded window. Prying it from its locked position, I slip through the glass framed fixture and easily allow the slab to descend back into position before latching. Leaving me secluded on the side of the lodge at nightfall.

Touching tips of my hind claws to the shingled awning below, I take no wasted moment of descending to the hardened poured walk below.

On all fours, a renewed nocturnal rush pulses in my veins in this graceful return to the feral. My spiritual will is now overpowering to break in run the moment of paw contact with the outdoor soil.

This hinting at my ulterior mood change; is there a chapter in the DSM-V to explains this?

SCENIC 7

The stone molded path is colder than ever beneath my flesh pads in a touch similar to solid carbon dioxide. Why am I forwarding outside overset with a fever this extreme?

Nausea passes between my stomach and brain like a full circuit coaster on overcharge. To ignore these added throes, I rest at a rotted stump preparing for what arrives in the form of an energy bursts coming to my gain and throttling back on foot, lifting off in my quad limbed ache.

Never before has lunar light caused a glare rivaling the rays of diurnal. While I acknowledge the wilderness is a feral, dangerous environment lurking of gargoyles. The rural is my dwelling as much as the enemy.

Instinctively and unwillingly, my paws lead deeper toward the hills and into the cliff meadows. The thick growth gives way to the shallow fields now bathed in moonlight's gorges lunar glow. This white illumination increases my head pain from migraine into an entirely new throb.

I do not collapse in the shade of plant or stone; some forex between psyche and body institutes to presses on. Exactly as my beloved ally Lolive, motivated me to force body forward against mind in completing that risk entangled leap. But it is not her memory of advice, nor her brother's. What is this empowering instinctive reaction having not surface before now?

As though I am high on endorphin, I find my paws griping the arrival of a cliff face. With agility rivaling the aptly name inspired Sciurus niger vulpinus, I free solo instructing each of my four appendages in safe vertical passage. Fear of losing grip or plummeting is not a factor slowing me down or to the point of prevention. In only moments, I pick up this climb in the shadow leading to a summit basked in the light of night.

Halfway, a numbness forms at each one of my digit points. The next grasp leaves off with a snap of the keratin. In this sensation, the pain is minimal in comparison to the height achieved. With claws broken under weight and natural cliff face, I continue upwards on energy only my mind challenges as nonexistent. Nearing ever closer to the summit, more claw points snap in pushing off the next foot hold. The moment my broken nail tips ascend the surface, I use the remainder of energy in heaving my exhausted form, to be greeted by the illuminating crescent blinding my visual like multiple organic lasers. It however does not send me over the edge, it rather invites me.

Positioning on my keens, I spread arms to welcome it on this young night. As feverish as my body radiates, especially in conclusion of the hefty climb, a numbing chill passes over quite similar to a chilling breath.

Yet the one action on my mind right now, is rest; in order to make up for today's tracing expedition. Before lowering head at point of nose, I remove my torso and leg garments. Folding together the garbs into a bundle catching the collide of my head. Having attained slumber in identical location is a rarity, as variety and location aids my form in gaining required rest.

When comfortably settled over the clifftop stone, the thermal feverish sensation arises its return. Solar energy is essential for external nutrition; does benefit exist also in lunar light? Regardless, a basking sleep presents a unique, grandiose experience. One I have not attempted, but willfully obliging to.

My night visions are plagued in sights I surely will not remember once they conclude. Upon the approaching end, all seems to be fading away into the presence of all colors; white. Everything loses its contrast and depth to every visual shedding away into blinding glare. The one and only escape is to awaken . . .

The blind becomes my paws forced over my parting lids. In a matter of moments, I adjust to the brightness over gradual exposition and returning to reality.

The illumination delivered me from slumber as never before, like a natural spotlight ordering the awakening. To go against it is my reaction, collapsing with back turned against the sky crescent in shielding my tear forming irises. On my belly, I regain notice of the head pain having yet to cease. Why does it remain, as well as the trembling chills throughout the rest of my form?

Reattempt is futile in returning to sleep against my managing return to the crescent at its full height. Now however, I hold it in sight with ease of minimal strain. A grand vista, clear and absent of clouds. Presenting an individually strong outcome to this awakening.

The hooks of the semicircle mimic a pair of white talons clinging to the sky for grip on its nightly ascension. Tracing its climb, I raise a paw to grasp it at the hook, where I am presented in a silhouette most foreign. In contrast to this lunar glow, I find a thin loose dressage clinging to my paw digits; hanging from the tips on all sides as an anomaly in need of closer inspection.

Raising the opposing appendage, these thin strips are as familiar as when first acknowledging their organic formation. Warm fur and black flesh; now dead, torn, limply hanging from my paw in pelt shreds. My claws broke in the climb when I attributed stress as the reason. Feeling no pain in the keratin barbs braking off, the now hypothetical scenario is contradicted by the reality of talons breaking forth . . .

Scaled digits of crimson topping off with strong claws at the points, bursting from beneath the flesh once my living own. Molting to a new identity . . .

Now my heart palpitates in newly arisen fear into what I am becoming.

Drama is a rare case in my personality. Complaining is useless in various circumstances having fallen upon me. When an irreversible outcome arrives, I do not whine and whimper on how it all could have been prevented. I bluntly accepted it entirely, shedding tears for a loss to be triumphed over in recovery time. Now I savor the last of my remain, as now are the final moments of my vulpine body in the molting shed of tear and fur.

"How, how did oyle infect me. Is the Dragon's Plague strong even from the exhales of another's reptilia lungs?" Whether this cause remains a mystery or transitions to a conclusion, I am assuredly forming into gargoyle.

The fever, nausea, pain. Each have the same unaccepted cause I never wanted to take upon.

"This . . ." Is a biology I cannot challenge, for it has already won. The feeling of this new body ripping out from beneath rivals a contained pressurized bomb. The heated steam building up with nothing to cap its expansion. My entire new form is aching to be released in immediate relief

How similar this must be for a reptile hatchling more than ready to free itself from its embryonic enclosure, an organic barrier in need of braking. The tips of my newly attached reptile claw points are the one appendage without an ailing tremble. Giving the digitigrade paws a second look over the intense sharpness that got me here, I have found my tool for the time.

Taking left pointer claw to my opposing arm, I pierce the sharp tip beneath the fold of my hide, tracing it up my arm in slicing beneath the flesh. The organic garment retract from the reptilian imbrications loosely as its expired time has unwillingly arrived.

My arms being free from the sleeves reveal the birthing creature; a crimson scaled pair of limbs to a body only a minimal percentage complete. Refocusing to my hind paws, I find them segmenting their maroon scales reflectively from layers beneath. Capable of fooling anyone into the assumption of gored wounds.

Placing thorn like tips into the scars, I hook beneath the tarring scabs to begin stripping my legs. Early into the action, a new sensation begins to form at my hinds into working off the skin; a swelling coming over like a throbbing fluid filled wound. The desire is to grasp in a preparation brace, but the pain intensifies to such an extreme I collapse belly up with feet raised against the crescent moon. The sound and throes come on que in a hart stopping occurrence. The bones of my hind paws snap forward, from beneath my dead leather they expand out into the hide encased paws of a gargoyle. Tearing away my canid feet to shards now hanging in strips.

I drop my legs as though just completed a sickly amount of lifts. But my newly found desire of freedom persists; bringing me back upon haunches. I feel the ankles before sighting them with my eyes. Scales here are of rougher design for endurance against even the most malicious physical contact. When prying away the remainder of my vulpine feet, I cannot but help grotesquely admiring the build. It has the mammal shape and form with an exterior enshrouded by the hide of cold-bloods.

As limited as my muscles are in vulpine form, I am feeling their heated pulse pressure against my skin in overheated layers. Continue this phasing, I must.

This time, I take each of my claws and line the skin fold around my ankle for secured grip. Without concern for pain, I fold it back to an instant coinciding relief.

My tail aches to an outgrowing extension were I retrieve the final moments from behind. Here I grasp the signature spinal extension I have known from birth. Its memory serves even from the black pelted days as a newborn when it was disproportionally short. Behind closed lids, my undeveloped eyes could not view, but I felt the expanse of my spine much like a fifth appendage

Long into its lengthening and molt into the warm colored fur beneath, I knew that this fluffed tail is what diverts me from other canids along with pointed muzzle and ear. Desire is with my dehydrated eyes to shed in full regret of lousing not only the signature genus trait, but most defiantly the final vulpes tail in existence. The lone individual to witness the departure of the subspecies canid is that of whom it is attached to.

Grooming it with gentle reptile claws, I find a rip forming at the tip. Index claw ready, I prick the scar and ease it down, slicing the tail flesh in a drapery fashion. I do not even reach the root before the throe transforms from pain into agony. With instinct of unknown source, I flex my tail back between my legs, raising it to the sky in an extension accompanied by a new slicing sound. The cramping spasm of my tail root is what intensifies to an unbearable endurance as the original root proves quite diminutive to a reptile's.

This feeling is a sensation I define similar to an explosion. Again my skin and bone expand, tail ripping open like a swelling limb pumping hard with muscle. I roar out in a vocal not that of a vulpine in raising nose point to the night sky. Hunching over in heaving lungs, I grasp the stone beneath while shifting bone and associated muscular vertebrates burn away their infliction. When it has made a finale of a passing, I move my paws to the new feature. It is close to the thickness of my new legs, but concealing a weaponized strength I am sure could rival an equine's hinds. A number of newly arisen points line the spine extension; upon closer touch and inspection, they reveal as newly bone extruding horns.

The entire lower half of my form leaves me burning with the same fatigue that brought me down over cold stone. But as much as I am aching in the newly formed reptilian pelvis, it is my torso and head presenting an overall irritation. Like wanting to shed layers of cumbersome garments, the remaining vulpes half of my body pushes to continue for concluding end; and end my mind is also pursuing.

Rolling belly down to move my claws to the shedding just below my scaled clad thighs; I rather take a pointer digit and slice it in a line up through my chest and onto my throat line. My disintegrating hide now feeling leather like amongst separation from the scales beneath.

Included with the new surfacing is an increasing shoulder tense evolving beyond discomfort. No reference or guess is needed for proper identification. Whether the amount of my control; I am sure it exists against any limit.

Upon quick instinctive decision, I make a horizontal incision over my neckline to separate my untouched vulpine head. Finalizing at the spinal cord and before retracting downward; a shoulder throe descends me into a returning quadrupedal collapse.

Each of my limbs topped with a paw has existed from the earliest moments. Other than spine topped horns, a new feature approaches. One desiring to spring as a nest bound fledgling. Feeling for the flesh of my lower back, I begin prying to release the same throbbing shoulder blades.

Pain is something I have known well for a great amount

of time. Dadyv and Lolive brought forth muscular tension when I made my first non-stop mile. Resulting in the discovery of just how much my physicality withstands. I fought off my mind to overcame all expectation of the body. But can I do the same now for this new side? Can the reptile overcome the mammal? Can the wasting vulpine be overcome by the ascending reptile?

I am recalling the time a strip of duct tape was laid over my muzzle as a cruel prank. There was the thought and attempt of easing it off with precision, pulling one hair at a time. I however, was moved into another motive action. Rather than dealing with the pain progressively, I tore the strip to endure all at once. Left with an uneven bridge of hairs paired with relief at how much easier the alternative was. I overcome the fear and belief in my limited tolerance, all because Dadyv ordered . . .

". . . Don't think bout it, do it!"

The fear is present, the hesitation, and the concern. But it is these exactly I must fight. In the reminisce of the duct tape, I pry up the dead flesh from my shoulders. Crunching at my ribcage with outpouring shoulder blades, my arms tense outstretched to the sensation exploding burst from my upper back. The remainder of my torso flesh severs in a most gory sound to the roar escaping my bellowing lungs in a howl I nor the chords of a vulpine could produce. The vibration from these new lungs trembles the entirety of body in an impulsing sonic burst. As a bow delivers its power to its arrow, my new form vibrates all energy into the cliff my paws clench against. I am sent into a deep beta just a hair away from unconsciousness. What keeps me awake is my impact over the stone, slamming against it as would a striking raptor. Not alone in this decent, two flat folds land on either side, draping over my forelimbs hot at the touch. Why are my arms so overheated and swelled four times their size? Yet with slightly parted eyes to regain focus onto my right paw, it appears nude in identical crimson imbricating scales. Definitely not the same overheated limb I am feeling.

Should I not be astonished by the sensation of this expansion? Why I am confusing my arms with another set of limbs? I knew only in the beginning what was happening, now it is as though my body and mind are attempting ratification. Slipping my limbs from beneath the inflammatory drapes, I bring them together in binding to reassure they are still there and absolutely functional. Pushing my aching form up, the drapes actively fallow limp, creating a flexing pain in my shoulders. There is no delusion in growing a third pair of limbs in formation of throbbing wings attached at shoulders. To the extent of wishing not to dwell any further, I begin flexing the newly fresh muscles for the first time. The memory of taking my first quadrupedal steps return in just how painful the first use of my legs were, and how time was the lone cure. Weak and genuine, these freshly formed appendages prove absolutely functional and full of the new life I am entering into. A life without an ounce of optimistic view.

For some reason, the rays of night appear far more intense than before. Moving me to open the new fingers of my limbs in a cramping of joints to shield my eyes, I cover myself in the leather drapes in ever intensifying fear of what I have become. Eventual hot tears spill from my eyes but do not make contact over my nose bridge. Immediately, the reasoning realization forms.

My scale paws touch fur when making direct contact to my facials. I am still vulpine from the neck up.

The burst of my wings left a great split at the spine of my head. Using it to my advantage, I take either side with paws ready and pull the leather mask down over my nose and muzzle with unexpected, welcomed ease. Miraculously, my ears remain intact. Yet when I can no longer move them freely, gripping reveals a tapered pair of horns at the scalp growing just above.

If I had a mirror at this time, it would most certainly

reflect the vision my paws are feeling. Even in this light, I know I am imbricated in crimson with reptilian scales cold and bare as if my fur has not been shed but sheered.

Naked, I am recalling to my birth. The previous time I was limited with a short haired hide. But is this bleakness present because it is gone, or on the cause that I have become cold blooded? My visible breath in the night air steams past my lips indicating I still retain body heat. Whether I will adjust my core temperature ever again is most uncertain.

Having finalized this transformation, I am at a stalemate of where to carry on to.
Dehydration is the one factor contributing to my lack of moist eyes. Clutching the naturally formed stone beneath, I so desire to be inanimate stone as the creatures are associated with. My desire is to storm into their midst launching every accusation. This vulpine is trapped as a hybrid now restricted from the minimal life he accepted.

Removing myself from my hide shards in proceeding to the cliff edge, my new eyes have properly adjusted to the rays emitting from the sky. The same casting over during the slumber, a rest that altered my entire existence. The desire is immense to raise muzzle in protesting roar of woe and disgust of being used. There is however no point of complaint. The amount of my despise weighs on my accepted the change, knowing there is no irreversibility.

As the true loss of the dog abandoned, my mentality sinks the reality into my new body like an imprinting scar untreatable. Am I feeling villainous, as I exclusively defined before tonight? For I sense more like an unwilling victim. Is the option of Oyle a lie, are mammals purposely and secretly infected? Am I the result of the manipulation?

SCENIC 8

The refrain to remain awake forms a paradox with my lack in interest to sleep. I want to be neither, existing only in a reality so exclusive that it does not even parallel this one. Why am I existing as an unneeded predator? I just went gargoyle against my will, adding an even deeper dread of being alive. Why could I not have been extinguished as a mammal, eternally expired in the last generation?

The remainder of my mammalian psyche burns out the last of its sanity while my conscience is extended by a jolt thrusting eyes open with a dazed sensation at my frontal lobe. A quaking magnitude passes throughout the cliff's entirety, accompanied by an uplifting tremor immediately forming into a repetitive pattern of rhythmic beats, much like . . . steps.

The next occurrence is the sound of two great nostrils inhaling directly from above. My own nose picks up the arrival of a deep earthly scent with a seasoning of raw gamey meat.

Thankfully, it smells only of unguligrade.

When the beastly point of the muzzle hooks my side, I am rolled over on my new wings, delivering a self-inflicted crush in pressuring fresh membraned joints. Grunting in the addition of this disgust, it quickly nullifies when I realize what has keeled me over. The great horned head above of neither mammal nor gargoyle doesn't escape my knowledge. Rather it summons an inducted memory like importing an ancient artifact.

A Dragon.

"I heard your birthing roar," she relates, "young gargoyle, I welcome you out of the molt. Hymnock is my title; and I offer myself as your inspirer." I am extensively unmotivated to respond or conceive an answer. In fact, a wholesome sensory claim forms in onset of a bizarre siren like audio-lock between my brain and ear.

"New oyle," the female declares on a most gentle whisper of a breath. The ringing is no delusion nor of external origin, it is present and increasing audio with momentary buildup. The pain expanses outward from my cranium as descent approaches, claiming every form of consciousness.

Night visioning from memory can either be relieving or traumatizing. I have experienced far more negatives in my duration. Only on a rare unexpected occasion does my mind conjure up a pleasant somber experience. Now is a time I welcome most exceptionally. This is the same warmth I had before being terminated dead-cold. When my eyes had only been open for a short time as a kit, I visualized with limited depth-perception in making out colors and shapes. Despite having no idea what to think or even understand.

Yet, I did know someone at the time by touch and scent alone as sound and sight did not yet exist in my biology. Knowing her meant life, only through her could I carry on. This was back when I wanted so, before losing the desire all together.

"... Fox ..."

The new sonic energy pierces the flaps on either side of my head. She comes into view as my new dark spheres present to identify her by more than touch and scent. But the feeling caressing overall is the intense warmth. Equivalent to an inferno of biological origin when my diminutive body couldn't hold its own.

The hardness of the ground beneath is surprisingly radiating with heat that would match a low-structure furnace. Yet the touch conveys it is pure natural stone supporting the body I am remembering is no longer vulpine.

Opening the spheres, I pray have not lost their blue, I am presented with blackened stone contrasted by fresh morning light. The touch, however, prevents me from arising into the cold filtering air, protectively ensuring I keep instinctively close the radiated rock.

"Awake?" comes the same voice from the last night I remember. Flexing my gargoyle neck results in my horns scraping the beneath. Grunting in the pain it grants, I find an even more alien voice than I last had.

"Guard those horns," the draco advisably warns, "freshly grown, they need time to firm up their strength. Don't even think you could ram on your first transformation."

"Why would I be moved to doing so?" I ghastly inquire in vastly altered voice by coming upon haunches.

"Are you not eager to finally become gargoyle?"

"It was never in my desire. I was infected somehow against my will."

The female counteracts, "Passing oyle into a mammal without their chosen consent?"

"It was not administered," I promise. "I am sure the contagion was passed from one's airway."

"Incorrect," she neutralizes, "oyle is the one way of

passing on gargoyle.

"I have absolutely no faith in you. To the extent of my knowledge, you reptiles secretly want us mammals 100% converted. Am I not the first to be manipulated?"

"Young gargoyle, you are as misguided as an arrow with a stray fletching. That is why I have volunteered at your side."

"I am vulpine! A sub-species canine bearing the title, Fox."

"Fox," she acceptedly claims, "you do not fathom your delusional and astray path."

"Then do not imply what is fact without evidence, show and direct me to the truth," I demand.

"Now that oyle has diffused throughout your body, you are illuminated in the night and enshrouded at light," the dragon details while urging me forward at the points of her rugged claw tips against my tender skin. Back into the night, we are greeted by the white light descending from its height. The same that put me to final rest as a vulpine. Now I am sighting the ever-expanding land with new reptilian eyes feeling no different as opposing my canine. Yet, the pair of my shoulders feel split with the newbie wing addition. Deformed is the sense they stimulate; protruding out, hanging limp like a pair of organic drapes, proving difficult to motion and only adding to the sourness of freshly born limbs.

"You need to use those, goyleing. Having maxed out into what feels like immense burning fishhooks, the one cure is therapeutic use. Unlike the avian, your flight pair are mammalian much like chiroptera. A pair of large membraned paws are the exact definition."

A part that retains is my lack of interest in questioning even the most extreme. Why do I care about what I am not responsible for; why is the obvious answer forming in direct communicative response with my mind?

Flexing the four of my upper limbs, they arise in an "X"

formation mimicking the photosynthesis of a flower's petals. In the same voice I do not recognize, the stretch at my shoulder line makes me howl in a burst of a snap. My large membraned hands open on retract of their digits like a hatchling reaching past its eggshell. I am feeling them, my new paws, lengthy, slim, and alive. They indeed are weak and cramped as if still enclosed behind the embryo, but I cannot refrain from this newfound biological sensation.

Claiming the rock surface of this mountain side, I settle upon reptilian haunches and bring my horned serpent's tail around placing its point between my knees. This mountain face continues radiating its intense heat even here out in the night. Yet it is not taking long to put it together with the consistent groan coming from in the earth. Deep and possibly too close for acceptable comfort.

"This is a volcano?"

"Yes, Phlogiston Appetite," the pure reptile confirms. "A mountain I know well, named for it everlasting grumble, as though it cannot ever satisfy its hunger of geological growls.

"Trust me, Forjah, a newborn never wishes an awakening to a cold world."

Managing to withdraw the limbs of my first birth, I individually challenge to independently motion the new ones. Snaps and pops accompany their decent to either side of my body. But here, now acting like two sails anchored at either of my shoulders, they appear like welcoming drapes in the night air. Two large leathery hands ready for a welcoming embrace. But whom are they welcoming? For they are weak in the waning pain of their new life, using all they have to engulf one who will accept unassured. But it is I, the receiver without chosen response.

It is before me holding out its welcoming paw, not offering a bargain or option, but all and everything it has. I have lost all of the vulpine life in only one night, coming into this new life in denial, lost and alone. There is no choice or alteration, no retreat, only nose forward.

Eyes sealed behind their retracting lids, I raise nose to the sky in a confident inhale as the reptile accepts the dog into the folds of its great membranes. Only my mind is conscience, but blind to reality with all my physical sensory blocked by this mystical energy cradling me in weightless zero gravity.

SCENIC 9

And how he dreads not being able to return to Escape or to socialize again. Not informing him of the mammal gargoyle reversion, on the cause he must first accept himself as a hybrid.

I am in the first moment of realizing the transition out of rest, as my mind has proved incapable indefinitely of recalling any stir. But this awakening proves different in what is physically felt. Why is my tail thicker, and why is there a sensation of four arms? But as instantly as the reasonings return, I ignore the remainder to arise in bedding not my own.

"Forjah, I must claim this is a most extreme change. Only

the previous evening you were a vulpine in complete denial. But I assure you, it is no guilt to me or any of my companions." Even with my new ears, I distinguish and recall this voice from the newest file mentally stored. Orienting myself in direct interception, I find the source identical to the one I first met. For the corresponding corsac seats before me, bearing the reminiscent voice of . . .

"Dixon?" I meet in my newly toned gaping maw.

"Your new body is going to need much rest," he advises. "Just as your kit body needed to develop into a dog." Now I am not withholding any amount of force by bursting from the bedding in his direction, only to collide with a transparent slab dividing the two of us.

"Be thankful your mentality is of soundness. Have you not questioned how your sanity remains coinciding with your consciousness?"

"He is correct." Confirms my mind as it comes to fully realize. I am enclosed here in this artificial cavern with a fright beyond anxiety, yet not without control nor tempted by a hungering instinct . . .

"As you witness your appearance, you are at a lack of expressing savagery." I widen up my facials like I would have when a desperate kit is in need of extensive revelation to combat the onslaught of an arising questionnaire.

"What you know as gargoyles, Forjah, is their blood thirst. Yet with a limited amount of will and no concept of morale, they are referred to as "Locoyles.""

To what amount of my own will does my trust take?

"A healthy mind and body are aiding in your transference. Such a head start with maintained oyle is a most pure advantage of hybrid development."

"My health benefits this alteration?"

"Absolutely vital to the same extent of nutrients." His clarification brings back the night's moment just before I was carried on the dragon's back.

"Though the diffusing oyle, soon to be your own, rages instability. There was no daring alternative opposing your housing here in these isolation chambers."

The quarters are of a neutral color scheme with only a cushion centered where I passed out. It even reflects my

RISE TO REHABILITATE
Understanding that Locoyleas
are the true enemy, those with
the true knowledge accepted
that Locoyles must be
rehabilitated in order to return
life to form.
A new solution was needed
to hunt and capture the savage
counterparts
The fur and scale
Hybrids are the answer.

monotone attitude to the point of counteracting any amount of emotion pouring forth in the moments of concluding my molting.

"These chambers are reserved for captured Locoyles in need of rehabilitation. The same enemy is wrongly associated definitively for every mammal-reptile hybrid."

Removing myself from the ground level, I find my legs quite functional, but keep the new limbs limp with only the smallest movement at the shoulder. But the slightest angle of my head toward Dixon stimulates the same ache I am becoming far too familiar with.

"Don't rush your change, it cannot be done," he insists.

To flex my scaled naked arms and again feel small horn nubs where my ears previously were, is beyond rejected imagination, a status I wanted gargoyles to remain at. A lone reality of speculation passed off as irrelevant importance. It is like when I first saw Escape before it opened, never anticipating employment. Then I requested an outdoor position before unexpectedly receiving the title of go-kart operator, the highlight of our recreational attraction.

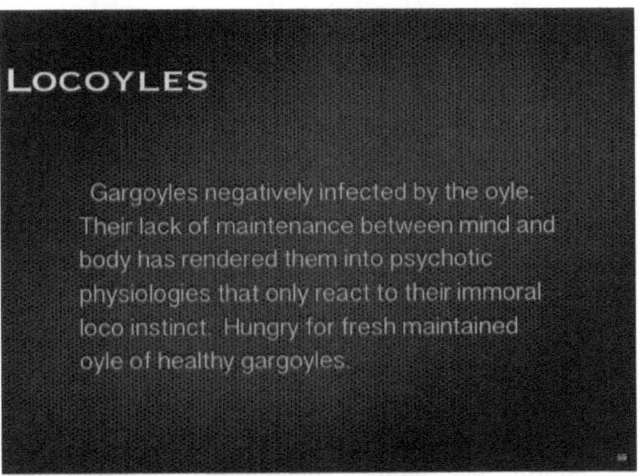

LOCOYLES

Gargoyles negatively infected by the oyle. Their lack of maintenance between mind and body has rendered them into psychotic physiologies that only react to their immoral loco instinct. Hungry for fresh maintained oyle of healthy gargoyles.

But now all is much like a savage de-ja-vu making its creeping return, waiting to strike. This loss taken from me is further milking its abiding, which alone is close to nothing. This drain began when she was taken, followed by his death, and now my dropping on cold stone fours.

"I've lost all I had," exasperating to Dixon. "Deprived kinship and now of genus. The inherited image now a grotesque dead end." Collapsing to ground my paws is the only sane action, hiding me in their partial darkness to grant the smallest chance of reality departure.

"Forjah, I am sorry to hold focus in the present time, but this enforced change is immorally culpable. We persecute and protect from those who act in such immorality, which is an alliance shared with your sire."

Does this make sense to me, is it penetrating past scales and into my intaking mind?

"Don't comparably define me," I warn. "That reptile . . . "

"Hymnock," the dog inputs ". . . from my birthing night has earned my trust; a challenge you have yet to equally triumph." This will drive announcement shows externally in my held expression as I, the newborn gargoyle connects eye-to-eye with this lead. Despite my heavily morphed facials, he knows an honest individual of my standard.

Beginning not with a vocalistic response, he extends forth his paw on the end of its limb in my direction. I meet the tips of his claws with my own, seeing my crimson shade basking in unnatural illumination. Dixon then retracts his arm and places paw over chest.

"At your desire, let us not be friends. But at my intention, let us not be enemies." Imitating with precision, the tips of my paw prick my chest just over heart. Who and how can I define enemy from ally after learning of the evil impurity that is Locoyles and not hybrids as a whole? Why is my mind losing into devoid of judgment to a vague tune feeling instinctual to a flight over fight? Even if Dixon cannot be defined as either cause or caution, he can be defined as the next route in this trek of a biological progression. There remains much to learn of him and gargoyles, and his advantageous presentations are inviting.

Dixon sends a request to a young whelp, who returns in a span of time my head is too fogged to calculate. Immediately following his approach, he passes a folded bundle into Dixon's paws who accordingly rests them over me.

"Garments of a newborn," he details. A pair of short

leggings and a sleeveless torso piece. The two assist me, a task of challenge exceeding my expectation. The garment is carefully slipped past my head-horns and to my neckline. Sensing my arms are next only proves wrong when I am instructed to first situate my wings.

"Fight the pain of your fresh limbs, they need it for oyle to circulate."

In a close relation to having a pair of blades removed at shoulder, I flex the membranes inward in a bellowing roar so alien coming from within this once canine body. Dixon and the pup quickly thread my bat arms through the seams, followed by slipping my original arms set into the dressage.

"Come, Foriah," Dixon requests, "you have been forced into our reality, now we are to welcome you accordingly." Like some repetitive cliché in filmography, I know there is no option of turning back to the life abandoned. Only the future is key to succeeding the present, all starting with my first move."

Arising with their inviting assistance, I follow the respected figure into the delve, where I first was introduced to his world and society. Beginning with a lead of a cavernous stroll, I follow without question, concern, or complaint. As it is a motto to accept the insanity and move on.

My talent of memory and detail in observation drew welcomed praise, as I am now documenting as though that appraiser was never taken. The delve is constructed underground so gargoyles can escape the dangers of the natural illumination. As I learned so long ago, it irradiates them into nothing with an incineration I can only imagine as utter agony.

Yet there are shafts in the roof of the great cavern that most certainly lead to the above-world, serving here as ventilation passage. Up there on the surface, it is nothing but avians, reptiles, and the remaining mammals.

But here among the gargoyles is every creature I know of in society. Acting together in perfect union in what I only know as sworn enemies. Could gargoyles exist here without them, because I have always believed we contently functioned without these reptile-mammal hybrids.

"My paternal beginning, he dealt in gargoyle rehabilitation? And his mate?" Dixon takes no pardon in my first question, but with turn of an ear, perked head in my direction.

He resounds with, "It is best I narrate your wonder with our first beginning. Retelling it chronologically, unlike a film plot arranged how the studios see fit."

"You are knowledgeable of such modern entertainment?"

"Cinemas are rarely ever illuminated outside of an emergency, Foriah."

Delving deeper down the path into the details of the delve's structure, I realize we are descending down the great root as thick as an aircraft hangar, wrapping down into the same earth yard I came to on the first encounter.

Perspectively, and with a new pair of reptile infused eyes, the delve grants an atmosphere most inviting to my cold oyled vasculares. Even the wood-carved path supporting my scaled pads entices me forward in the trail's descent.

As my attempt at supporting myself in the gradual incline proves uncoordinated by the addition of my membraned limbs, Dixon offers a supporting paw for aid in the balance. His provision is most appreciated in part due to the daze holding a cling to my mind.

Holding my head suspended from its sore clavicle, my motioning hinds almost need my parted eyes in aid of making the steps. Yet what seizes the attention are the array of den-like nests aligning each side of the great root. Passing the opened mouths, I catch the sleek-surfaced objects enshrouded by torn fabricated strips of multiple weaving. Yet, sharing an equal purpose: warmth.

Sheltering over the swaddled eggs are the scaled and

cold-skinned creature into which I have unwillingly transitioned. The hybrid sires and dams, overshadowing close to their unhatched offspring are protective and sane, awaiting the hatching of those succeeding mammalia.

The construction of the individual dens is quite remarkable; appearing to be anything from a tent to full wooden-framed shelter. This is only the outside however; for they are literally carved into the wood of the root for extension of the settlement to shelter and grant needed depth for the inhabitants. Some have even carved their dens so specifically, the concave is an obvious use as the overhang for an additional shelter-like canopy. Specifically, each of the dwellers have constructed these nests by use of salvage. A low tolerance of build quality assured, it is an exact opposition of how my own sire had to carve his own den to win the appraise of my dam. Similar to the legend involving a dragon building a hoard of riches to win a mate.

How then have these hybrid parents courted each other with makeshift carvings of a den? Has the downfall of mammals reduced the honor and respect only previously obtainable by action?

In this new body, I am feeling bare and exposed despite the hatchling garments. Trotting with these legs grants the sensation of attachment like a pair of prosthetics. My new membraned limbs are at similarity with a pair of dumbbells pulling on my internal shoulder ligaments. Yet on the more emotional level, I have not seen my image since this transformation. Here though, every gargoyle and mammal take this newborn's image into the windows of their minds with complete . . . acceptance.

I am not a rejected deviate, not in any sense on how my past life would view. A contamination, requiring to be dealt with accordingly. Above, I would be confused as the enemy. Under earth, I am welcomed with open wings . . . gargoyle wings. They know I rejected them just yesterday, seeing me as the threat of danger to their race of companions. But now amongst their imbricated hides, I am further accepted accordingly.

"The same force that destroyed me as a mammal and a vulpine, is granting me the one and only option of a province."

SCENIC 10

"Double!" I demand in hot ready pursuit of assaulting my target. The cub obeys and tosses two discs in the air now sailing toward me. With adaptively trained reflexes, I hurl myself forward on the spring of my hinds to meet the projectiles in the air. Hurling with a spin as my organic foot collides to the first, and the second with the foot of my spring bar. Leaving them warped in meeting their final match today.

"Anymore?" I request to the Acinonyx cub. The tom declines so, meaning we have concluded the session. Presenting the cub with some disc currency, I briefly appreciate him on his departure to spoil his earnings. Why does a kit want something in return for taxonomic retainment? My inspirer was never this way, never once charging a gamut.

Looking over the cavern field, I take in the image of our past heroin perched upon the stage. Many have removed or swapped the dried blooms that once beautifully lined the memorial images. In an unforeseen number of calculated days, the material respect will be retired along with his own departure.

Blindsided, I discovered he left a son who is irrelevant to Taxonomy. But the quite stern non-influenced nature of this dog not only proves his lack of interest, but that he is instinctually deviate from his biological origin.

Wrapping the attached rope around the steel bar, I sling the trusted tool over my shoulder and decide to take in my inspirer's memorial one last time. Ascending the steps with a drooped and dragging tail, I settle myself on knees before the bouquets. The dried withered leaves remind me of myself, a dead wilted individual who before bloomed with life. Resting body here as a flower no longer clinging to life here in the dark cavern where the sun cannot touch and nourish my vitality.

The only living irises here, are the ones dripping tears over my muzzle. Am I to continue drying up, parched and decomposed? Life has not provided a clear trail, and I have not put anything forward. As much as I desire to remain here mourning, I must ascend to Escape for the interview.

The great lodge is what now constrains my interior surroundings with the occasional stone either assisting or decorating the structure. I made my private entrance through the locker room in the tranquility of the morning leading up to the gate withdraw during the first shift.

Slipping through this doorway may have been stealthy, if not for the lupine draped in a dark cloak over a brightly colored torso garment signifying Escape's uniform. The varg's expression is welcoming of my entrance into the vaulted corridors.

"Vision?" she assumes with a gaping yawn. I formally confirm by dip of muzzle angled at tilt of neck.

"This way," the lupine directs with a raise of her fashionably draped paw toward the hallway's end. If I am to pass as a domesticated vixen, I must practice a behavior with equally the same amount of respect. Not once question or wonder and so imply inappropriate prying.

"Obliged," I appreciate with sight set forward into the dome of Escape's mansion interior.

"I am Losse," greets my escort. "My commander has been expecting your arrival. On the fact your own is a college of his, you have a distinct advantage in the interview."

Stepping under the arch and into the central "A" frame, we are greeted by the lodge's belly of concrete flooring. Log stacked walls and planked balcony's surrounding the inner landings.

"Escape?" I inquire with a raised brow. The larger canine hums a low moan like a minuscule howl answering with, "Our Escape, serving as our own recreational destination. How else would we keep our sanity with multiple whining young, non-mammals, that is."

"An extreme stress reliever," I summarize.

We head to the opposing side of the lodge, where I am guided through a doorway to a settled room bearing a display of a window overlooking the complex's exterior grounds. Without an added vocal to lead on into the next step toward my interview, I approach the glass pane to view the outdoor attractions. Directly out beyond the doors is the fountain adjacent to the indoor natatorium. Trailing the walking paths and into the far south are the two opposing go-kart tracks, separated to serve both inexperienced and mature drivers. The discus course spans out on the grounds western-side to coincide its scenic river and obstacle layout.

All looks so inviting in comparison to the deep in the dark underground. Flaring up is a rise of my zerda tail in reactive excitement without diminish even when another enters the command room.

"Vision," the masculine holder introduces in a spur of positive mood.

"Yes," I verify in return. Finding a woodland brown Nyctereutes procyonoides entering past the threshold into our midst. The coon-like beast offers a bench rest which I formally accept before delving right into the interview following only a brief introduction.

"I am commander Clevarest of the recreation destination, Escape. When seeking another set of paws for the establishment, your resources and my close alliance forwarded the recommendation. You are obviously interested now, so please Vision, grant us your qualities so we can clarify your fit to Escape."

Delving into detail of my physical and intellectual experiences, I further back up my skills and capabilities in relation to the type of positions Clevarest has set for his crew. The males operate most of the physical requirements of the park's exterior while females focus on the more disciplined requirements such as interaction and cognitive obstacles. As much as I prefer the physical action, leaving it to the males forms no loss as plenty of labor exists in the Delve alone.

"I'd like to hire you, as long as you acceptingly agree without intent to form regret." This may be a blunt statement, but the sarcasm really lightens the hard fact in a gentle engraving. Extending out my paw to this domesticated commander, he meets it in the air in formal contract.

"In accepting this position, I thank your approval." Whether or not that is respectful of a domestic vixen.

"Welcome aboard, Vision," he embraces with a canine grin. "Losse, if you will please show our new crew member to her station and dormitory." This black lupine once again takes the lead, showing the way as a new colleague. Having allies are difficult back in the Delve, but Escape is feeling different in exact opposing fashion.

We ascend to the balcony in the lofty second level by encircling around in a complete passover. Its southern end beares a greatly detailed window with view of the recreation center's front gate while the north opens out to an external landing overlooking the highlighted grounds I just viewed from Clevarest's quarters.

West and east of the upper level beare a variety of doors, some ajar and some withdrawn. Losse's destination is one easily distinguishable by its heavy bulk of a wooden slab, which forwards on hinges as we enter in. We are greeted by illumination, both artificial and natural, bringing the den to life. Aligned against the wall's sides, suspended from the ceiling, are cloth- and rope-woven hammocks individually placed over assortments of chests and bedside wardrobes.

"Our dorms serve little purpose other than relaxing," my lupine co-worker relates. "Clevarest wanted them to be just that when he acquired the land for creating Escape."

"Can't imagine any alternative. There is too much here to be confined to dorm in the diurnal duration. I'd call it nothing more than a rehab period between activities."

Losse returns from a near walled closet with a folding of strong fabric and synthetic tethers, a hammock.

"You are already accommodating well," she praises, while passing it into my paws. "This job is as social as it is tactile."

Choosing a pair of hooks close to the window overlooking the grounds, we string up the net and test its strength with both our weights, finalizing the strength when she and I find we are able to hang from either of its ends.

"You now need a unit for your gear. Come, we will find a fitting amongst the storage."

Behind a door only paw steps down, we enter into a room with no windows and only an archaic incandescent bulb up top appearing ready to burst. But the pure canid between the two of us does not even bother with flicking the switch on for the reason we share distinct night vision. In moments, I catch a wooden chest capturing my attention. An oaken wardrobe speckled with dust and scuffers, presenting wear and age.

"Having a limited arsenal of gear, this will suit me." Tilting the heavy end toward her, the lupine raises her arms to catch its lean. She volunteers to take the heavy being the larger of our species. I take my end through the door first where she follows my lead so not to damage it or the door frame.

"Losse!" calls out a vibrated voice of one who is ascending the stair flight with wild speed. The two of us temporarily set the wardrobe over the planked flooring as the holder of this call completes her approach. A lioness.

"You, Vision?" the cub inputs with assumption." Jade is my official title.

"Crew member and roommate?"

"That's right, dog," she incorrectly defines with a forwarding of a paw. "Welcome to the crew." I accept the feline's natural tool into that of my vulpes.

"Being of the female side, I am classified a vixen."

"Much like us Lupine," Losse inputs. "I am called a varg like my mother, while my father and brothers are termed as dogs." Jade's ears sulk in a hint of guilt for the misjudgment, and in the exact opposite of our canid fashion, twitches her tail in irritation. But coming along side this in an unexpected jump. She retaliates . . .

"Taxonomically, I am lioness."

"You are further building my confidence in being employed here," I involve in attempt to resurrect her spirit while taking up the wardrobe in assistance as the vixen helping the varg.

"Save your energy." Jade insists on taking my place." You are new and need to learn our duties." I am giving no objection to this matured cub before willfully giving up the burden. At my size, she is not quite fully matured, yet possesses tremendous feline strength in the task at paw. Physical leonine prowess is attributed to her bestial inheritance.

"Jade," I ponder to myself," it is not time to reveal just how extensive MY energy is."

SCENIC 11

This tour of the delve briefly ends as we move from root over to earth. I have granted Dixon little questioning, as I see it somewhat pointless being now I can only accept what is here before me and what I have become.

The memorials are been removed and retired, as he did long ago; just as my vulpine identity. Never being a gargoyle, what does he think now that his lone offspring has transitioned? Before many of these thoughts expose my emotion beyond control, I blurt out in whimpers, draining fluid from my tear ducts in elevation of pulse. Dixon reverts his head on me as would a gun turret locking on, eyes wide and rounded like a barrel.

"Foriah, many know us vulpine to be so . . . adaptive. It is an advantage that assuredly carried in your transition.

"It hasn't quite set in," I admit. "I just want to preoccupy my mind by putting the smallest amount of ease to my spirit." The dog heeds my proclamation without challenge or hesitation.

"As a fresh newborn goyling, your speedy desire for involvement is most unusual."

"I want no time to think. I just want to act." This finalization of my stated need gives Dixon the conclusion he accepts. With a raise of each matching wing and arm, he guides through a tunnel anew to a destination I am defining as undesirable.

A draft of fresh air hits me in an inhale of the underground trenches. I begin picking up the familiar sounds of domestic animals making their rounds, vehicle engines, and many machines I have heard before.

"Are we below?" I guess in accuracy.

"Accurately observed," Dixon comments.

"I also have another." I proceed onward, "In all this darkness, how are we managing to not fall into the Vayl?"

When we arrive at a brick wall, I take it as a dead end. Just before assuming we are confined, Dixon hoists up on the protruding bricks to begin a vertical climb. I tail him up with uncertainty of what to review this experience with. Somehow with this freshly transitioned body, I am astounding myself with its added strength as an influential assistance proving pleasurable.

From within this dark shaft, the city outdoor sounds begin fading against our ascent. Soon, it is only the scrape of our claws against the stone adding to the tranquility.

"Utilize your wings, don't think, and only act," Dixon recommends in disciplinary. "Climbing will build up their strength."

Having a limit to calculation, I feel we have climbed a great height far beyond what I thought possible. But this wall is most generous in holds for each of my paws, almost as if they were deliberately designed for such an embarkment. I withdraw my wings from their locked position and raise them high over my head to feel the protruding bricks as the second pair of paws they are. Hoisting up is still a ways, but I can maintain balance by securely gripping with my thumb claw points over the holds. Dixon is right in moving them, compared to last night when shredding out from my former physique.

"Grant yourself the time required to build your new body with newfound strength. You will know and will easily learn its developmental pace."

The depth gave this wall a chilled touch before warming to the touch. I have limited ability to tell exactly how high we have climbed, but a glance down only shows a dark pit presented in night vision. There is no light here and my eyes have only gathered a small amount.

"Nearly to the summit," Dixon calls from above, "where you are going to learn more than you know or anticipate." This totally is obliterating any response I had ready, yet I desire to not retort or present any question. I can however, forward my acceptance.

"Looking forward to it," I present.

After this repetitive haul, the corsac halts, holding strong over the bricks, right beneath what appears to be an iron-slabbed top. When an obvious unlocking sound clicks out of place, he heaves the slab up on concealed hinges. Opening into light instantly flooding what remains of my sight. I grunt how I never could have predicted against the stiffening firmness clutched by each point of appendage.

"The night welcomes our arrival," my guide instructs. In his direction, I forward up into air fresh and pleasingly wafting. Of course, this moment is only lasting a second as I see where we have made our way to. Seeing my new-found concern, Dixon offers his paw, which I take against all thought process and helps me onto the ledge towering among the many steel peaks. That entire climb was up a concealed vertical trench alongside this massive sky scraper.

"Welcome to the heights, Forjah. We are getting high in a much more fashionable alternative to many others." His declaration is true yet with an equal amount of humor, but my mind's one focus is having a back against the wall without a toe or a claw over the edge. Diverting my mind may only be of minimal assistance, but I must act outside of my head.

"On the optimistic side," I observe in my personality, "I'm glad we are not out here during the light, I can't imagine being incinerated."

"Are you in wonder of why this vertical passage exists?"

"That is just one of many," I open up, waiting to learn even more." My feelings remain and suggest there is much I misunderstand and even more absolutely unknown."

"You Forjah, are adaptively perceptive. I know you are far from your paternal in any maternal likeness, but I assure you are unlike anyone to ever be infected."

"Present to me," I confide, "answer my concerns and ponderings, and provide the missing keys to my mind's empty spaces."

We exchange a bow, followed by his lips passively presenting this new reality.

SCENIC 12

To a cause remaining unknown, mammals lost their ability to biologically reproduce. As the race's entirety dwindled and diminished, we found ourselves few in number absent of joy in expecting new generations. As alone as each of us felt, we were not so. Dragons optioned as responders who attempted and failed to cure our prosperity. Though it was unsuccessful, they offered an alternative creation (through natural magic) called the Oyle. Which regenerates and heals our organs, returning the fertility to our bodies. But in order for this full effect to "heal" us, we could not be brought back endangerment spontaneously. Oyle made our bodies new and reformed at the cost for prosperity. Making us into mammal-reptile hybrids: Gargoyles.

This motive proved to be absolute controversy, despite entirely elective. The dragons, nor anyone force this on the barren. The great reptiles had succeeded in granting all mammals a solution, but had failed to concoct what was desired. No one fathomed laying eggs hatching into scaled offspring. Optimistically, reptiles had done their greatest and continued searching for a cure; without a conclusion.

Negatively, there was no preparation for what spawned out the mammals begging for a cure and the reptile's response. Creeping up as if from a mad lab in a dark alley, many gargoyles turn fierce and psychotically begin preying; hungry for blood warmed meat. Rumor built into plague, accusing dragons of corrupting to create the Oyle. Infecting mammals in forming gargoyles as the self-inflicting extinction for the remainder of mammalia.

Chaos was the only form of order. The psychosis infused instinct of the locoyles drove all into panic, leaving the nights deadly and rendering the solution as accursed. A new discovery surfaced of how oyle burns unstable in what was originally warm blooded vasculares. Yet, the onslaught of the predation instantly distanced who we viewed as our saviors; defining all reptiles among a class of traitors.

But betrayed by the falsified paranoia, the gentle giants were not to leave us. Recent findings uncovered many were gleeful in accepting oyle to an opposing extent of what would in time be referred to as locoyles. Connections were finally made after much observation revealed the chemical as unstable in the vessel of an untamed gargoyle. Foreign yet effective, it pumped hot and overbearing to the physicality and mentality. This ultimate discovery zeroed in to find that a hybrid can maintain sanity with proper maintenance of its oyle.

The next goal resulted in the move to capture and rehabilitate all infected. Strictly, reptiles resorted to not only stabilize gargoyles, but jointly training them in the conducts once exclusively their own: Taxonomy. The taxons allowed us to become what was never intended outside that of cold bloods. Much like a pact, they agreed to form us into Taxonomists.

Leaving our part to capture and rehabilitate.

Is there a part of me actually viewing satisfactory with the gentlest touch nudging me forward to satisfy my temptation at the smallest level? I don't know what is true anymore, but I must begin somewhere so I can compare it to the wrong.

"Conduct, philosophy, and interaction passed on through a biological infusion."

"Even the dragons cannot provide full explanation on how it works, as they did not expect gargoyles to inherit just from a biological source." Dixon points out.

If I still had my ears, the would be perking in this spark of curiosity. But some of the dog is still left within me, for I motion my tail in excited preparation to learn even more.

"Our physicality changed so extensively when transitioning, that our biological response drastically put forth an unexpected result." Dixon's declaration is not of a regretful memory revision, but mere pausing with pure awe I never will be able to distinguish on a gargoyle's expression.

"Not only do our bodies regenerate our fertility, but they began regeneration by giving life where never before found or existed. We gargoyles had more than traits of the reptiles, we had an unforeseen unplanned miracle. Our new life forces gave life to inanimate forces. Literally sharing it by granting manipulation to previously nonliving forces in the form of an extension from our own paws. This is what we refer to as the ultimate miracle of mammal and reptile emergence."

Dixon's bringing of me to this tower ledge has endowed me with more knowledge than a full gargoyle conspiracy could suggest. Being put on mental overload, I am panting while fighting my own mind's reject of disbelief. Dixon easily is picking up on exactly what is going on in my contradicting head.

"As we endow life upon what was never alive, I have laid much info upon your brain that was always dead on what exactly is true."

"Perfect description," I praise.

SCENIC 13

Returning to the dark tunnels of the Delve is relieving considering the great heights, as the gargoyles refer to the sky scraper summits. My vertigo has dwindled, but my wholesome entirety will not forget the power of gravity. Though I know the more I focus in tune, the greater comfort will develop. A priority now that I am half reptile. To overcome as I learned to maneuver a track filled with high speeding go karts.

Yet now that same line continues in my head as a mental recording never to cease. Some of the strongest advice ever received, began back in that abandoned quarry, when Lolive and her sibling Dadyv urged me to follow by diving off the edge into the water-logged mineral excavation sight. The drop is most likely a building height to the surface, where the siblings awaited my decent. So much was going through my mind, I was unsure what to listen to or ignore.

But Dadyv called from the waters with, "Don't think, only

act."

Exactly that, I hurled off the cliff edge with nose down and tail up, hitting the water quite smoothly. The depths brought me under while I breathed out at the moment of being submerged. Rising up and surfacing, they congratulated my accomplishment while I marveled at where I leapt moments ago.

At that time, the water caught me. This night, it may have been the two appendages, no more than two days old. If I had lost grip up there before the scape, could these sails have caught me? Would I have instinctively reacted, or allowed my end to carry out?

Of course, the greatest occurrence of this evening is receiving Dadyv's exact advice from another pair of lips.

"Don't think, only act." I did not stop Dyxon that moment, nor approach him before turning in. Whatever the formatted connection is between them, I am instinctively holding back in dire hope of independently discovering it. An indy direction to carry out to conclusion.

I am reentering the Delve inversely. Dyxon suggests I take rest for the remainder of the night in accordance that it is equally important for goylelings. As a pure mammal, my vulpine body matured toward a dog nearing his developmental completion. Now being reverted to an immature hybrid presents itself in a sensation of retrogression rather than advancement. It certainly won't be a developmental ease, proving comparable even in an absolute alternate body.

My ears pick up my approach of the Delve before my eyes receive the light. Passing between guards, one rodentia and the other a pale slate gargoyle; the reptile-infused creature makes brief visual contact while I trek on. Not sure now if I would rather be what I am now, or a dog in assistance to gargoyles. Just as my sire was; but as unlike him as ever, I remain.

Currently, as he is on my mind, I should quite possibly

retrieve his gear from the Escape locker, as it just may be the limit of my material past. I do not dare returning there as much as it pains me.

"I can never associate with them. They may be blind to the reality that has been revealed to me, but mostly to me no longer being mammalian. It is as though I have died." Yes, Forjah is gone. Infused by an unknown source, yet not infected into a locoyle. Yes, whoever poisoned me must have failed the transition into a villainous psycho.

I could at least visit Escape in the evening hours in making sure all is safe. Now I can imagine the only danger is them being attacked by the locos . . . wait, what if I can do exactly that? Yes, we gargoyles defend, why not be posted at Escape?

"Then I would assure it is at peace." I will never lead them into the dark as I can never again enter into their light.

Locating a record den and acquiring a diagram of the tunnels; I am instantly overwhelmed by the vast amount of passages, forming inscribed geological trails like an outline of the circulation system. It is like a map of a mammal's nerve system with varied color-coordinated branches.

"Smart for a hatchling to study our underworld system," comments a female civet whom I had passed upon entering the records den.

"I was forcefully infected," I correct.

"Son to our alliance," she defines," you are a hatchling considerate. Apart from the cause of not breaking from beneath eggshell, but out bursting mammalian flesh."

I had not thought of that classification, yet I theorize she may be right. I hatched from a dying barrier in order to reach life.

"Is that the common view of the immature gargoyles?"

"Absolutely, whether skin or shell, all goylelings shed into identical conclusion. Acknowledge assuredly how the dragon's gift was horribly turned into a delusional curse, the same delusion that limits my trust toward a newborn roaming free."

If I still had my ears at the moment, they would be raised to the stretch of their points in reflection of my astonishment; yet my new reptilian facial characteristics seem to be substituting just fine along with the droop of my tail, hanging limp. This cat is immediately detecting it, and with a brief apology, rephrases.

"It is still quite early to be labeling any judgement upon an offspring to our alliance, but a major purpose of a gargoyle's advancement is to determine you are not foe by gaining the trust of each delver."

"Please," I plead in an attempt at slowing her pace, "should that really be my primary goal and focus?"

"Priority is what you must make use of; build your life here in the Delve. Dig a den, retrieve any possessions, and build on the advantageous aspects of the life you have been offered exclusively. Yet remember we, your allies, are the best for info far exceeding that of a leather- bound document."

There is simplicity here with the promise of deeper details, but this new education is evenly balanced, challenging my left brain hemisphere. I will never lose the feeling of another at my side in my mammalian end, I could not have been welcomed by any other.

"Hymnock . . . "I remember, "she named herself my guide."

"Ah, the dragon responding to your birthing roar. She will be a sort of foremother instructor. It is she who will be at your side in your progression through the Vayl, natures, your role perspective, and especially the taxon of your choosing."

"She was the loner to greet me into this reality. I feel I owe her."

"In debt to your guide is a powerful thing. Strengthening our bonding with the scaled beings who healed us and our future generations."

Hymnock will receive my thanks, yet now I must take

action, preparing a place here in the Delve, for my life as a gargoyle. The past must not weigh me down as I instinctively might react.

"Which route will take me to the Escape locker room? I desire to retrieve all belongings from there." She maps out the correct tunnel connections in only a quick overlook before directing me to the corresponding passage. Satisfied, I thank her and depart. Making Escape a destination one final time.

Planning ahead, I do not bother even glimpsing into the closed vault interior when retrieving the gear, which I stuff into my own pack as though erasing the past: the life that was taken from me by that unknown being.

I do not give a single concern to removing the lock and keeping the door ajar to show my former crew mates I have made final departure. It is best they never know, as I have officially been made into the misjudged enemy.

Hoisting the pack over my shoulder, I close the hidden door latching in place, severing the final connection to this once-delusional life.

In these dark tunnels, I am soothed in a security I could never conjure in any mindset. The reason may be that it pays homage to where I was reared, in the hollowed cliff from the moment of birth. Now that it has claimed dominant subject of my mind, the more my desire builds to return.

"YES!!" I proclaim in my act of discovery. Poring over the same cartograph of our underworld tunnels, one stands out, isolated by branching beyond into the forest outside urban limits. Memorizing the exact route proves quite easy following a few repetitions. Toward the western mouths, tail and wing trail in my sprint.

I know I am in my destination tunnel by how far it carries on with no alternate passage. In the dim of my night vision, a stone set of steps turn upwards in the wall marking the trail's end. Spiraling up the stone steps, I take caution considering the smallest chance I misread the map.

The carved ascent tops out at a definite wooden slab serving as a door leading to the hope of my estimate. A single iron knob is fastened to its top, which I take in my paw and give a turn. It responds to a pull in reveal of garments hanging on a horizontal bar. Sized for a mature dog or vixen.

Reaching past, I push the opposing doors on it arms to proceed past the attire and escape the wardrobe, arriving at my birthing den.

"All this time," I outcry, while glancing in every direction before returning to my point of entry. Retrieving the rest of my gear, I then return the false rear into position with assurance I can return. Fidgeting with the single hook proves it indeed opens the hidden door with a single turn simpler than the combination design. Respectfully, I place the uniform into the wardrobe.

Greatly fatigued from the day, I decide to look over his gear after a complete rest. Setting it alongside my own, I then remove my newborn garb and set it aside. But before closing the doors on their individual arms, a reflective surface on the uniform catches my eye. Taking it up, I find it to be either a round mirror or glass disc suspended by chain. It briefly catches the lunar light filtering through the den's skylight, striking my eye directly.

Passing it off as having no idea what it is, I return it to hanging position and seal the enclosure. Completely and suddenly quite warm, I curl up in my dugout in allowing sleep to consume my entity.

SCENIC 14

I return to the steel heights alone, with no guidance. There is absolutely no control over the gravity as the paved streets rise to meet my plummeting descent into accelerated terminal velocity.

The asphalt comes full detail, far too in depth for my mind to conjure. The sudden emptiness of the streets is an eerie visual; nothing and no one to witness my demise. My body remembers the sails, but the dragon limbs are non-existent, having dematerialized without pain.

My will is to black out before impact. Will it be enough to save me? Up until this exact moment, I was fully insane not knowing reality from fantasy; but this delusion is dying out and making a return . . .

Chills thrust me into consciousness. Scents of the deep earth touch my nostrils as my paws cling to the soil beneath. It is as though my body reclaims neglected breaths as my lungs heave and inhale, wheezing in pain. I have no option apart from forcing myself up to give the cardio clearance.

Once calmed with a fresh breath, I collapse and return with elevated pulse. I thrust my backside painfully on the fragmented debris I left from my kit-hood; but I am ever fueled by adrenaline as a realization hits me this exact moment. Rolling over, belly down, I give a flex to my shoulders to find nothing: no third pair of limbs.

On my knees, I run my paws together to feel the familiar coat of fur, my vulpine pointed muzzle, bushy tail, and ears.

"GHA!" I pant out in awakened relief.

"A night vision," I specify. To wake out of this vision is a true savior from the reality of my terror. To think my immediate acceptance to a new life was instant. If actual, I would have grown accustomed, formally being a creature of adaptability.

On my canine hinds again, I sight around my familiar birthing den, unchanged and undisturbed in the early rise of dawn filtering through our soil-clad skylight. Now is time to return for the early risen go kart riders, preceded by a satisfying meal.

Yet even before I approach the den tunnel, I am thinking back to the vision when I placed the delve uniform within the wardrobe. Padding over the trampled stone floor to the cabinet, my paws ease up to touch the cold metal of the handles. They click apart at the lock, before I immediately thrust them back into place.

"It was a night vision," I remind myself by crawling down through the tunnel and into the moistened woodland. Nothing beyond an extreme yet mystifying mental conjuring of slumber. Certainly an experience worthy of novelization. An envisioned reality I released from, possibly by will alone. A Chimerical Escape . . .

To stride over the concrete path to Escape is joyous after a long sleep, for this feels comparatively closer in actuality to that slumbering sequence. Customers are spending their usual wait before the entrance gate, eager for recreational action.

"I am well ready to receive business."

From outside the garage, I hear both Trident and Ares firing up the engines to warm for today's run. Causally passing under the withdrawal door, I take up the golden arch kart, choke and yank the pull string for a confident sputter before returning the lever back into position.

Ares' crocuta head comes up from behind the headrest of our #310, alerted by my entrance.

"FORJAH?" He calls over the roar of the engines.

Bowing in a likewise greeting, our calls signal Trident, whose puma ears perk up from around the engine rebuild he has certainly made progress on. Once firing up the last kart, I meet him at the work bench. Despite my limited engineering knowledge, the block is almost identical to the gasoline exhausting engines warming behind us.

"A rebuild to a high percentage," I comment, "you assuringly will bring #12 Mantis back on its axles." Other than its muffler and pull cord cover, it may be ready for a returning mount to its frame. Yet Trident's focus diverts from the machine, despite paws bearing a socket drill and equating sized bolt. Meeting the tom face forward, I find it wide eyed and muzzle dropped open, my attention drawn to the assembly of confused looks.

"Trident?"

Ares appears from behind the karts, his mood not so different.

"Your moods are most disturbed?"

"Dog, your location for the nocturnal duration?" Ares scoffs in detectable sense of bewilderment.

"My home den," I reveal.

"Your place of birth." He rhetorically picks up a location known only by your mind's intel.

"ARES!" Trident roars over the exhausts to invoke silence form the hyena. There is temptation to criticize the hagine for prying so, as I intend to keep the dugout concealed as did the sculptor.

"Forjah, being we are mammalia's last, going incognito . . . gargoyles, you know, getting exsanguinated."

"I am as thankful as you are." I argue in preparation in case leading to a bickering. I so wish everything gargoyle was created out of my night visioning to every ounce of my willful desire. But oyle remains an accursed lie of a gift by dragons. We are what is left of the furred creatures, in total absence of ever prospering. I believe there is no cure to the unknown cause of our infertility, yet there is optimism calling back to the alternative I unwillingly imagined to equal the extent of being infected against all will. Before passing, to record the mental experience in its entirety, presents fine fiction for creatures remaining here after

"You're right, brothers. Deviation is dangerous, I'll be sure not to repeat the mistake."

After flicking our switch box and pulling the repaired karts into the station, I head up to the lodge for much desired morsels. Trident insists he and Ares will catch up as soon as he mounts the engine block.

Feeling I have little energy to burn, I trot instead of sprinting with the need to reserve as much as possible. Passing Jasmine as she lays out the discs in the shack, the puma jumps at the sight of my approach.

"I have returned safe." I reassure the molly. She gives a gentle nod with the exact fright Trident and Ares granted.

"They really care for me." I memorize this pleasurable fact now retaining in my psyche.

Here in the awakened morning, I find the lodge quite cool amongst its tranquil silence. Passing out of the main landing, I make way to the cellar where our private bistro is located.

Sloping down the ramped hall, the trailing scent of oat cakes calls my emptied belly, offering the primary of my physiological needs.

Seating myself at the bar, I await the nourishment with every ounce of patience. Losse and Jade have the morning meal duty, Neon will take over the lighted hours, then Ares and I have the night. The varg and lioness prepared much to accommodate the crew, yet I do not see my preferred quencher. Being the one to favor it, I am obligated to prepare my own. Pumping fresh water, I fill a cylinder before adding a serving of cold tea; both healthy and rehydrating.

"Forjah, mind withdrawing the maple sap?" Jade requests while filling a saucer with pork from the grill. I give a bow and proceed to the cooler. Losse is powering down the fryer with those long flowing garments, miraculously devoid of any soiling here in the galley.

"DOG!" She barks at my presence. Closing the door reveals her on the opposed side, scrutinizing me like a watchdog.

"Varg!" I respond, feeling as she apparently does right now. The lupine bears an entire platter of hot cakes, easily drawing away any attention she just had. With the maple spread in my paws, she shuffles her massive pads in my trail to the bar dividing the lounge and bistro.

The sound of billiard balls clacking together seizes my focus as I realize a new recruit is among us. In Escape garments of black, is a vixen of gold strikingly contrasting her attire. It is a balanced level between a harvest and breaking diurnal rays. Unfortunate one so fair exists in our approaching extinction.

Neon is challenging her as stripes where she nears to sinking the eight ball. The vixen seems unfazed by her upcoming defeat, being that Neon is obviously less mature in taking on the newcomer.

Once Trident, Jasmine, and Ares arrive, Jade and I have little time setting out the saucers before Commander Clevarest addresses to the cellar.

"Come crew." As we gather around the bar stools, "our newest recruit has come aboard. Vision." He introduces the golden fennec who is replacing her cue to the rack.

"Delighted to be a part," she announces, "your crew, Escape, and its guests."

"OUR crew," Losse corrects.

"You're stuck with us," Trident sarcastically teases. "Welcome to the team." The two exchange a clench of paws from feline to vulpine, and everyone follows by either greeting by contact or just a welcoming wave. I simply grant bow to which she responds with simple dip of her muzzle.

Completing our introductions, we each gather around the semicircular bar to refresh ourselves for the day ahead. Everyone continues chatting with Vision to expand their knowledge and present her with how the shifts flow. Yet I am too preoccupied by the maple-soaked cakes literally melting in my jaws, granting the calories to empower my mind focus over another vision, my night vision.

It felt real, but there was also a supernatural and otherworldly quality invoked by the vision. More than enough to fill a fantasy novel of immense unmatched originality. With only moments before having to head out to the track, I begin copying down the events in great detail. Writing up to the point of awakening in my birthing den, I have filled four pages of inked inscriptions documenting my endurance covering every point of memory.

As opening nears, we kart operators make our way out the back door with paws picking up into a competitive sprint. The station gate is where we await the drivers the moment Clevarest unlocks the gate. But even while making sure the track is clear and each tire is pumped, I clutch the pen in the pocket of my uniform and feel the other pocket to reassure the notebook remains. I am in pure awe that words can hold such power while hiding it at the same time.

SCENIC 15

     I'm in deep appreciation of the calmness the day exposes from the terror induced delusion. As a gargoyle, I could not enjoy the solar rays as it would incinerate me. This is the most favorable part of being employed outside for all the adrenaline bursting action under radiated rays. I almost pity gargoyles for sticking to the night, despite I should not have guilt toward the enemy. My apathy was put to extreme in an opposing battle with optimism. The extent of the falsified endurance, what genuinely remained even outside consciousness is the desire to end; joining the mammals long expired.

     The track is running swiftly, karts blazing their mufflers in the scorching heat. Along with our diffusing homeothermic bodies doused in fumes of the same fuel, burning in our sinuses.

We have little time for a water break between heats.

Though the bald designed tires naturally grip the track surface, spinouts happen at every turn; or as we classify it, a mistimed drift. This presents a struggle weighing persistently. The kart of a bestial driver spinning out, reorienting the kart by pushing up the inclined bank is a struggle. Many times, the delay of my response is enough for Ares or Trident to assist. The two of them are powerful by their species; leaving this lone vulpine at his limitation. As a traceur, I am adept at lifting only my body weight.

As the solar disc prepares to dip behind the woodland horizon, the heats of drivers begin maturing from the vivacious youth to the thrill seeking adults. Only two karts today needed repairs, involving a body mount and a loose fuel tank. With twenty-two out of twenty-four, we are more than prepared for the last rush.

Long before the night satellite shines its pearl-white spherical mass, we identify the shift nearing its end by the public thinning out and Jasmine closing up the discus shack. Vision and Jade, our newest recruits assist in shutting down the arcade and flipping off our open sign. When the final drivers are seated in, Trident gives them their rule call while Ares and I string the cable across the back rows to secure for the night's sleep. The last of the drivers launch out, and I am finally able to rehydrate by pressing a cool steel rim to my lips.

"I miss sleep," the hyena conveys. "Never thought I would. I hope for the possibility of tonight being peaceful. How long the duration?"

"Far more than an acalculia mind would bother estimating," the cougar determines.

"What is so important that it interrupts sleep?" I intriguingly cut in as the engines begin rounding their turns. The hagine barks over the muffler roars.

"An answer, Fox, that your mind has long documented?

It is no different than when we were kits and pups. They have always been there making the clouded skies and the shaded forest unsafe."

He is right, gargoyles. It is a miracle I only encountered them in my night visions. Unlike cowering in the arms of my dam and hiding myself beneath the mended covers of my den. There I would tremble and pant, hearing them outside in the trees and in the air looking for prey and any disastrous action they could take. It is like their instinct is pure malevolence, devoid of true purpose.

But these gentle giant reptilian facials, and individual creatures among them as friends in alliance, actually played upon the guilt I have just developed for my life-long enemy. It is a long standing shun of gargoyles as the feral enemy, and my immediate 180% turn would make all shun me.

"It is only a fictional reality conjured in my sleep." Words and literature are no threat to existence, for all should know to the same extent as I do about how dangerous the hybrids are.

Trident is alternating his observant feline concentration between the two of us with little attention to the last drivers of today. Into about mid drive, he begins cracking his knuckles and inhaling deeply to pant out in ruffle of his great muzzle. The race nears its end, I prepare to stop the carts with a motion of our caution flag. Waving them down, I follow their trail around the remainder of the track, only to be carried back to where my track buddies have remained. Ares now has a darker tone to his sable eyes, a sinking to his maw, and droop to his whiskers. But it seems it is Trident who placed this reaction in the heyenine.

The drivers pull to halt at our finish line in a perfect single file row. I love it when they do this, it is an easy task to load them back into the lanes, adding to the night of rest motioning forward.

Ares brings the gate open to signal for the return of their

modified mowers in the station. Each pulls into to their assigned rows in orderly fashion, Trident signals in loud mountain-lion projectile voice that all karts have stopped signaling; everyone may rise and exit. I bring the cable from the station post and run it through the headrest to lock its end at the opposing post. Once we kill the power to each of the engines, we each share a collective bow.

"Successful day," I comment, "time for what I hear defined as R&R."

"Rest and Rehab." Ares specifies in translating the acronym. "Is any part of you dire for it, Forjah? Your night was long with your absence and our concern."

Trident cuts him off with a reverberating growl, breaking what he meant to finish. This is good as it presents my chance for completion.

"From how I rested only the night previous, I want physical reassurance. To amplify what my mind commixed as to what can only be defined as an otherworldly delusion. My brain thinks beyond supposed capability when my body rests. Forming a power force of ideas both vastly original and of exceptional quality."

We return to our fellow crew members upon entering the lodge for the night. My track mates lead on either side of me, Trident setting his predatory gaze forward and Ares intently watching his toes touch the next set of planks in step. While I am documenting away with both sight and ink nib up to the sixth page of my notebook.

Locking the oaken doors behind our tails, we officially shut down for the night, our track now a dark shroud in shadows early made by lunar rays. Every escapist is pulling back our iron shutters over every window to the point we are clustered inside the fortress of our lodge. But as Ares, Jasmine, and Jade join the newest recruit before the door to our cellar, Losse and Trident remain behind in reaction to my holding back.

"Forjah, . . . I thought . . . "

"Survival attained," I reassure, "you are acting as would an over worried friend from a cliched movie plot." The lupine's eyes reflect that same emotional care we have had for each other since our first befriending. It is Trident who always held us together, in a way similar that I am the metaphorical combo of feline and canine between them.

"Filmmakers do not draw inspiration without a source." The felidea joins in. "Why not represent actual figures in one's own life? Though far off topic, she is in her right place as if a supporting character to a protagonist."

"Why am I dubbed protagonist?"

"Cause you are currently the subject of concern, as our lead dog." Losse's point is genuine, for I am the first to ever have been hired. Everyone looking to me as the overall guide and keeping the business peace.

Trident now indulges by enlightening with, "we mammals are in endless danger of further bringing ourselves to extinction. Our social trust is genuine to an extent we would only understand if it were taken from us . . . "

"We won't allow that to happen . . ." our varg adds as completion.

With tail limp and nose to the planked flooring, I take in the emotion of their meaning. Is my incredible story idea and distancing myself truly a worthy risk all for some personal time? After all, I value their lives far more than my own, yet it is they who really care about me. I met Losse when I viewed her sitting alone and isolated back in our education duration, Trident and I came together when jumping on the same subject of our beloved games. Our trio has since been a hyper coaster of out and back, always returning to our solid station with not one stop or derail.

"You were absolutely right to worry for me, but my experience was a grand unexpected happening that has forever accelerated me onto a trail I know to be true, just as the two of you are. I was rewarded with an inspirational idea so vast and original, I know it will fill an independently unique manuscript."

They are both congratulating me on the unintentional achievement as I am lead down the sloping tunnel into our cellar as the scent of raw cinnamon bread readies for the iron oven. Ares and I form the dough before coating it in spice and lining it along the enclosed surface of our iron pan. Loading it into the artificial heat risen oven, we take in account of the estimating time and leave it to bake.

I relax on a sofa with capra's milk meeting my tongue from the steel cylinder encasing. Jasmine sits opposite with Trident settled below, stroking the underside of his purring jaw.

Vision is taking her first taste of the cinnamon bread Ares had just introduced along with Losse, determining it is properly baked with no raw or burnt loafs. I am attracted to yet another game of billiards between Jade and Neon, causing my hinds to carry to the table in greater observation.

For the first time, I am seeing just how the two females play in a practical silent rage.

"You indeed know a strategic set of moves, but your lioness cannot counteract my animation." The tigress sinks two balls with such force, a spark erupts in a snap of visible electrical flare. "All you foresee is loss."

Static charge, I squat before the ball return, to find the 1 and 4 balls bear a matching black mark upon each of their surfaces.

"This is literally mentality versus physicality." Jade insights as I replace the marble like balls and retreat to the bar for some much desired fresh pastries.

Claiming a bar stool toward the end of the high rise, Losse offers me a saucer with the steaming pastry ready for my savoring consumption. I take it and press the spiced surface to my dried out nose before placing it over my moistened tongue to a much loved sensation of the substance in my canine jaws.

"You are Forjah?" The golden furred recruit inquires from across the polished slab.

Vision is a zerda, I believe; with her high set of long pointed ears and short tipped muzzle, the exact opposite of vulpes vulpes.

"Correct," I confirm, "go kart operator and soon your trainer."

"So it is on this turf," she challenges, "but in the depths, you dog, are the noob."

There is the option for explanation of the metaphor, but I see no need as it is pointless. So I move the conversation forward.

"Tomorrow at high light, I will give you a tour of the outdoor duties when Trident and Aries have the track covered."

"Approved." She confides with no additional feedback. This vixen obviously is set off by an external force. Neon was shy but opened up in time, Jasmine branched off beyond just being the lover of my closest friend, and Jade came in alone but quickly fit herself correctly into Escape. This Vision is capable of adapting, but failure to fit in will lead to her termination; which will prove its value in time. Yet she is off to a rebellious reluctant start. There is only one who can train her for the grounds, and I am that lone individual.

"Make sure to rest your body tonight," Losse advises to Vision, "the fem's and I are planning an overlook amongst ourselves."

"Go on then," Ares projects, "we have the uptown covered. The next I take down has no anticipation toward the wrath of my longing for sleep." Ares is just as exhausted as each of us behind his spunk, but I am in wonder what the hagine is doing out so late in the night.

"Ares, what interrupts your sleep?"

"Gargoyles. Every flight keeps us going on without end. I long for what I am deprived of." Strange how the creatures made themselves present during my outing. What value exists here in Escape? The last I encountered were in my night visions. Obviously they have kept my go kart companion awake with attempted intrusion.

Finishing my cylinder off, I proceed into the galley and clean both it and my saucer. Feeling some more ideas coming on, I am about to retire myself to the balcony when Losse shoots a recommendation to our new colleague.

"We will go when the light is just a glow over the horizon."

"Among mysteries I desire to be solved, it would be the explanation why gargoyles prey on newborn blood. In Ares' situation, never able to sleep as a kit is traumatically relatable."

A breath escapes me in relief, Vision had identical kit hood experience. Possibly providing an opportunity to build off tomorrow during my instruction. Lightening the feistiness of a new recruit can be at my advantage.

While the disc dips its last light beneath the horizon, I think of how I trusted the belief it burrowed its way into the earth and ascended again during the dusk. As creative an idea it may seem for a novel, I have my own new ones.

Claiming a tranquility relaxer atop our balcony, I take in the night's fresh birth into my welcoming cardio. Though only a porthole in concern for nocturnal safety, I give thanks for the design choice of ventilation. How it must have been before oyle, before our barren inheritance, to have a luxury of being under lunar light devoid of being the prey. A time I do not see ever returning to a new generation.

I have increased to a total of eight pages, while pondering questions instigate through my critical thinking process.

"If reptiles are responsible for attempting to cure mammals, is there denial they were in actuality, attempting full control by granting a false cure?" By far a great conspiracy spread throughout, but am I to retain it or be the optimist and present them as saviors? That may ruin it, for the true fascination of the lie is not knowing the answer.

"Exactly how here and now." Wrapped up in my composition to such an extent, my consciousness does not take in the thunder of paws until they pass over balcony.

"Forjah," The voice announces to be that of Losse. Looking up briefly, I give her a slight bow in attempt to multi task in conversation. Yet in my side vision, I see Neon, Jade, Vision, and Jasmine are accompanying her, each positioned in a perfect line with eyes each reflecting an on edge emotion.

"You dare risk a night unsheltered," I remark in referring to what they had planned in the cellar. Eyes and pen tip to the paper in assurance I do not miss thought or idea.

"Yes . . ." she starts with a sudden loss for verbals in an almost visible shudder through her jaw. Her voice has been diverted by the instant sound of a sharp point over metal. Immediately, I realize the balcony and the lodge are wood and concrete; the only metal near us now is the roof. Positioning my neck on a pivot, I make out a silhouetted object through the glass just past the overhang of the roof. Dark and completely motionless aside for that one scraping sound it failed to prevent. It is comparable to if I were to drag a needle over its metallic surface in a painful frequency of a sound. Yet this object is not the whirr of an exhaust fan or vent fashioned to atop. I see this balcony from the track every given moment, and I know there is nothing of this size and immensity atop.

Losse is directly between it and I, still not voicing anything as if struggling what to convey. Acting out of instantaneous instinct, I put aside my ink pen and notebook before rising up slowly to wrap both arms around the lupine to bring her close: eyes still fixed on the figure. Touching lips to the fold of here ear, I exhale . . . "Get inside!" The moment this info passes, Jade grabs Neon with clenched paws and forces Jasmine and Vision back into the lodge interior. Losse and I remain motionless as does the mass on our roof. She embraces me in following the act. I want to blast behind the safety of the log walls, but will our capable strike be enough?

As silent as all is now, I do not want to accept what breaks it completely. But I have found that nothing can be done about it. Just as I have no control over an ear penetrating cry erupting from over the grounds up above the go kart station. As if on cue, the shape on the roof opens its wings like a large leathery pair of pointed fangs against the light polluted sky. The dive is even more brief than the length of time between the glass shattering and its dispersasl, spreading out in all directions as Losse and I thrust apart by the beast's impact.

My descent to the wood suspended floor is blackened by the bend and snap of the tranquility chair beneath my weight. My sides are scarred from the lupine claws as I know marks of my own grip lay over her. But no pain can compare the emotional scarring of the creature directly overhead. Its scales of blue navy, wings of a deformed mutilated chiroptera, tail thick like a python ready for constriction, and aroma of decaying death reeking from imbrications to venting on breath.

It approaches me on all fours, positioning between Losse and I as a sort of barrier. Common among the creatures as they are territorial, not allowing a single competitor. My ally, she expects equal concern for myself. Though Losse is misled, I can't give primary focus beyond its menacing breath carrying closer with salivating jaws hungry for prey's blood.

In reaction with an unknown origin willfully empowering mind and body, I draw in my knees to curl up, appearing submissive. He takes the bait. When close, I hurl my legs out in a spring to return the favor of ambush. The reptilian mass hits the wood with multiple snapping planks beneath. In speed easily matching the force I just used, the others are on the gargoyle in a flurry of fur upon scale. Jasmine and Vision restrain its high limbs by wrapping forelegs within its wings while Neon and Jade secure its own fores.

"Losse now!" Jasmine orders the lupine, who needs no cue of command before joining the restraint. I have vague expectations as her black paws grasp the sides of the beast's head.

With strength I can't originally define, she twists it to the side before forcing muzzle downward to latch at the shoulder as would a Desmodus rotundus.

For several moments, they remain here holding the creature with every ounce of energy as my own fuels into my disbelief. The female crew members restrain the intruder while Losse assures a firm grip with jaws nestled in the scaled hide.

In an amount of time unidentifiable, the hybrid ceases its struggling before everyone pulls away to leave Losse latched to the neck by fang point. The gargoyle begins to breathe at what appears as a steady lung expansion.

"You are healed." Losse comfortingly expresses while removing her fangs and licking over the incisions for sealant.

The beast believed to be an overpowered creature of the night is restrained before me. There is nothing my mind filters to my tongue. What am I witnessing, what is taking place?

Losse, my reliance, presents me a look hard to read even in my night vision. Lips damp with the remaining drops from the creature's flesh, she knows I am seeking answers. Going this great while without questions, is it wise?

Before I even accept into it, his head breaks away in the direction of the doorway where Clevarest now blocks with Trident and Ares.

"Allies," Losse promises with gentle paws on either of his cranium horns, "you are safe."

"INSIDE!" Clevarest orders while casting his eyes in every direction out form the balcony.

"The rooftop!" Neon intrudes as we reassure there are

no others beyond the shattered hole. Losse's paw pressures on the back of my shoulder blade to pester me inside. I come through the threshold with eyes held over the intruder. Ares is unmoved by my total ignorance, equally comparable my lack of inquiry. But once on the platform of the second level, a thought returns to me like a lost treasure.

Trailing astride the railing in direction to our room, Trident and Losse call across as I latch onto the stainless knob before dashing into the darkened dorm. I clear the space of my hammock in only a second to collapse before a bundle. A stack of glossy plastic books in a good sized pillar, my console gaming magazines.

Paws over tile and forward over carpet reveal that of puma and lupine; Trident and Losse. My paws take upon a numbness when resting over the cover of volume 47, reassuring that what I am seeing is also physically present.

I arch my neck and meet the glowing retinas of my closest companions. They too see my eyes shine moist with instant forming tears. Here is a bridge, one between reality and visionary too far beyond.

My puma and lupine companions both raise me to a bipedal return. They mean to convey something informative, if not for a newly risen commotion erupting from what we know is the balcony door. The three of us don't think, we only act.

Abruptly stopping before the banister, attention fixates on the balcony entrance, where the high door has been forced open on now flimsy hinges. Only Clevarest and Ares remain, with everyone mysteriously absent.

Another descended gargoyle, much larger and of ink leathery flesh. Clevarest gains its full attention with arms wide in a taunt, while Ares partially obscures himself behind the drapes of the upper level windows. Just when the beast is about to prowl upon my commander, the hyena leaps and lands jaw first on its shoulder. Hynenine bites are among the strongest, yet repeating Losse's action is a reason I refuse to gravitate toward.

"You are healed." she conveyed. Never before had I experienced a night vision that felt unnaturally real. But now, my psyche is doubting I ever did.

The ink imbricated beast collapses knees first before haunching in reverberation of lodge platform. Clevarest makes his move and barricades the single balcony door. My hagine crewman maintains grip on the creature's shoulder, remaining in his prowling predatory pose. Now I am feeling there are many to-be answers I don't want established.

This time, I kick off the banister and propel over to Ares as he unclenches grip, leaving tooth marks with only a limited oyle loss. Oh how my mind would prefer to ponder this gargoyle's lack of iron.

"He's fine Forjah. While maybe not our friend, he is neither our enemy."

"Neutralized?" I rhetorically question.

"Fresh oyle," he informs with a quick tongue swipe over the amount on his lips, "even faster than feral itself." If I had time to process a response, I would do more than fathom the hypothetical form. Cause what is coming forth breaks our focus and our defenses, as an appendage with keratin barbs lurches through the door opening. In frantic response, I impact fully through the railing and descend out over the lobby. In reflexive action, my eyes and paws find the loose-limbed extension the same moment before catching the boardwalk beneath. The moment my pads meet the treated slabs, two more are coming down to ground level. How they got in instigates my flight induced instinct.

Reversing, I leap into a quadruped run for the rear doors for an escape. Briefly arching up on hind paw, I pry the slabs apart, jump kick the wood on its hinges, then bring the steel slabs together in locking the beasts inside.

SCENIC 16

Claim My End

Here I am alone with the roars I traumatically endured as a kit. The night is not quite young, meaning it is the peak of their time. The only entrance open is the balcony, as I can hear a few attempting their own break in like a competing quarrel. Out here, I can only choose in being useless.

Ducking out from under the shadow, I begin free soloing the windows directly aside. Too close by greeting of battle cries. When my ears are visible over the floor, I fold them down against my skull for concealment. Reaching in assurance, I propel off and latch paws around the stone structured pillar.

Our balcony is a cluster of gargoyles turning on each other for reason beyond me. One of the same color as the arm that burst through the steel barricade continues attempt to gain entry.

Swiftly on furtive paws, I vault onto the stone rails then through the shattered opening. Positioning directly above, I dive paws first and kick off its chest and return to my hinds in recoil. In timing relatable to my assault, he regains ground aided by chiroptera limb, colliding with me by shred of shingles, going up and airborne.

The only thing I am sure of is the force of gravity pulling at me like a thrill V coaster. No definite direction assures me, and I feel only the iron flesh penetrating grip of my captor. But despite the contorted surroundings and motion sickened body and brain, my instinct overpowers all. Clenching my teeth in preparation, I chomp into the smooth hide of the beast in repetitive snaps as he induces a comparable amount.

Concluding a fourth and final nip, the clutch of the flying beast discontinues motion as we are aligned directly head first to the ground. On impact, the creature collides first and my body bounces off like a spring board sending me into freshly sheared grass. Fear forces away nausea and dizziness as I align directly before my assaulter who remains dazed yet alert.

It too comes matching in quadruped stance ready for the prowl. I hear Losse, Jasmine and additional voices warning me to safety. I may not know their point of flee, but they know my location exactly; on the go kart track turned battlefield. My opponent snarls with a reptilian voice much like the one I heard from Hymnock in the night vision. He is taunting me in stance, ready to lunge forward and claim my end. To communicate with this psycho, I return with taunting snarls; sounding from my muzzle is a voice I do not recognize.

When only a kit, I would curl up in my stone dug den, hiding eyes beneath my tail as my feline like ears tuned into every gargoyle roar outside the security. I cried associating myself as the prey they sought. The maternal figure in my life would embrace me in reassurance they would not find us. I know this now, but all I could manifest was imagining how they actively looked, leading to a conjured visual most disturbing and vague. But here, on the kart track facing exactly what paralyzed my immaturity; my fears are in absolute control.

I am ready.

Propelling off hind legs, the gargoyle makes an identical launch to meet battle ready. Calculating the correct time of action, I ascend all legs with forepaws outstretched. My paws clamp around either horns, taking me down along with himself. Managing to roll his weight upon me, I give no chance and spring my hind paws to the jugular. Falling away, the creature dazedly falters with head drooped over chest in sense of a knock out.

This time, I withdraw my crimsophilite; extending the blade positioned over its left horn. He begins gasping as if attaining air for a first time. Raising up by arching neck to find me holding an unsheathed tool overhead, his eyes are changed. Looking emotional and . . . sane.

His collapse brings him down under the blade. Pulling knees into curl, it begins sobbing. I did not acknowledge gargoyles have the capability of weeping; in submission? Either positive or negative, I feel a mix.

SCENIC 17

With warning to my peripheral sight, the allies are descending above. I am now clearing over the track; vaulting the chainlink to land the opposite side in quadruped. Summoning the remainder of my adrenaline, my quads burst toward the barricades.

Clevarest retracts the sliders apart just enough for my access into the Lodge safely. He heaves it closed and I take the opposite to where we bring them together into locking position.

"Where are the rest?" I pant with heaving cardio. "The two I fled from?"

"Forjah . . ." the dog exasperates with a short slip of my name in frightened turned somber mood.

"Could any have broken above?" I suggest. But my commanding dog takes me by rest of paw over shoulder, leading me out from beneath the second floor overhang and into the artificial lights. In a warning of impossible prediction, the light fixtures go black with a glare in my vision of lunar exposed silhouettes fading away. Chills creep through me at the sounds of claw and paw over wood planks. The balcony door once again spreads open on its sliders.

They broke in.

Clevarest's grip remains clenched over my shoulder blade as he forces me behind his study door before sealing it between us dogs. An eeriness strikes me blindsided.

"Commander!" I project out in a bark as though howling to the moon looming over the glass corona high on the roof. Immediately, the sound of solid bodies thrust over the railings from the second level.

Securing my side of the iron slab, I back away drawing chrimsophilite at paw, extended to the door. I dare not voice out or make additional noise to draw the enemy. Clevarest, what reason exists to separate?

In vague attempt to control my breaths, the sound from the hallway presents in the form of a rap over iron.

"Fox," sounds my name in Losse's voice. I dare not answer. "Unlock the slab, I acknowledge your biological change." She is safe, fortunately. Yet plagued with what I deny, my instinct is to fight.

"No gargoyle broke our barriers," she finalizes the moment I pull the restraint bar. Recoiling back, I hold the blade out in preparation. Yet my nocturnal vision picks up her lupine paw thrust the slab open where she enters calmly. Though I am in no mood for chances, she is startled at the minimal light over my blades.

"Forjah." She sincerely voices with elevated pulse. Holding her paws up, she drops to her knees before me. "Your mind is not as it was," she pleads with moist forming eyes, "you and I extended a shared love. Though transitioned out of romance, it is love unchanged."

I give no additional thought, she has pointed out that I

am making myself the villain now overcome with guilt incurable. The clang of the metallic object hits the wooden planks in sync with that of kneecaps colliding. We succumb in embrace where I too begin shedding at sealed lids.

"The source, define what ails me." I force out through clenched jaws as her paw moves to my torso in caress over the bites received.

The varg signals for Jasmine, who enters bearing a satchel. I am forced over the planks as the molly quickly begins pressuring the wounds I am too dazed to notice. Losse cradles my head over folded thighs just before pulling her paw before my inhaling maw. It is dosed in my blood, a silver thick liquid devoid of any scarlet.

"This exsanguinate is cause for your mental and physiological alteration. Oyle," she describes.

SCENIC 18

The pulsating pressures over the sealant presents a firm reminder to the throb of my brain. The info it had formed and retained in what I wanted to be fiction, is indeed factorial. Forcing grip to my shielded eyes; I make no commotion upon being transferred to the upper level. This is to limit the most diminutive and minimal amount of contact.

The presence draws the hither of my crew, to which I give rise to my chest in assuring my survival. The angle changes to my staircase ascension before the comforting sling of my hammock swaddles me.

"Heal up," advises Jasmine. I position paw over the wrapped wound to grip the incisions in a comforting seal devoid of any red. To an extent, the feeling of never knowing my mammal blood sheds over.

"Fox," arrives the fresh voice of our commander. Clevarest hovers over my form in calming relation to a taxidermic figure. My colleagues and Vision position themselves before the doorway against his foreground position. What may be received from him now is most unwelcome, yet of the greatest necessity.

"You are under infection?"

"Officially." I declare to them and myself.

"Dixon confirmed," Clevarest states, to my lack of thrill to hear that name. "Reported you entered the delve a vulpine in denial, only to return the following as the first wrongly infected."

"My body . . . it reverts between both forms," he elaborates. "In the open this evening, you did not transition with only being in the lunar shadows. Also, the myth of solar illumination incinerating the hybrids remains nothing more. It only imbricates scale and horn in reversion to mammal form."

"I reverted?" I rhetorically output. "As unintentionally being infected."

"The leads of the delve, including taxonomists of presage perception; prioritized your acceptance. Once adjusted, your knowledge of locoyle and gargoyle would be broadened to the point of illuminated reversion and return here to the surface." The is no source of a response, as my lips prove unable to passively open and touch.

"The locker I presented you, the very one occupied by my dear friend; is your mistaken route into the delve. This discovery, led to your infection?"

"Most definite!" I shrill in a sit up against both the throbs of my torso and Jasmine's intrusion to lie and guard my form.

"Straining those wraps will only complicate your healing."

In my ignorance and focus to greater concern, I challenge, "is there a possibility of airborne contraction? Delayed inheritance?" For the medical time she endures, this feline is the one in proximity with the greatest chance of finalizing my fearful wonder.

"There is limited probability of either. Breathing the scent of oyle has no effect, nor is there a documented delay of infection lasting in completion spanning full growth development."

The ultimate desire presents in the form of launching more possibilities. Though in succession, they only complicate the theories into deeper pondering.

"I will not fully rule out any impossibility." The mate of my trusted tom ensures. "The focus must be forwarded into converging evidence."

Though it is vague, it is an extended comfort to reclaim sanity. Lowering head back to the cushion, it catches in a slumber temptation to my battle scarred hide and oyle pulsating cranium.

SCENIC 19

Days drag on as our invalid draws ever more distant by result of reaction to the infection.

Forjah has multiple times when needing seclusion so. Now the first victim to the cure of reptile's venom, he must desire support and guidance. This contemplative tone and emotion prove contagious as Jasmine nears my position in response to my pondering.

"Trident." She greets in reflection of similar mood. "Attempting to cool your head? I am the lone one who can quell a heated tension." Her chilled paws make contact with my scalp in delivering a tingling adrenaline spiked comfort.

"Forjah is never to be the dog preceding. In all form of his rejection to the oyle, this physical change has completely vaulted that unique psyche. Before, it was only closed, now it is sealed. I almost feel wrong to have kept all from him despite moral of self discovery."

"Gargoyles, like the dragons, are not a race of forced motivation. Imagine a more terrible outcome if it was forced on him."

"Now you are only adding to the pain."

"He has been victimized." She retells, "Fox alone is one to never manipulate. This dog is hurt at the emotional level and the first ever to be."

Slipping arm around the waist of her uniform, I pull the dead cold cougar close to further gain her reassurance.

"You remember Skylar?" I bring up the name Fox never uses. She grants a bow before I rephrase a line she had left.

"Even a cataclysm has fertile soil." A metaphor pertaining to moral meaning of advantage stemming from loss. Forjah is meant to be infected, and we are here to find the extended intention.

I am in no state of awe when he approves of running the track on his own.

"Anything to do with gargoyles and the delve is not my level," states Forjah before Ares joins Jasmine and I at the lodge. We signal Neon and Jade, who leave their positions at the disc golf shack.

"Your emotion has shifted," Ares points out with sincere hyenine focus of eye and ear.

"Caution Ares," Clevarest warns from beyond the the serving bar, "Li-Fan against another can be destructive from the deepest emotional level." The Nyctereutes holds his masked glare in an effective mood and the hyena inhales by intaking his savvied responsibility.

This was I admit, uncomfortable in the beginning. But it is I who trains him in the use of his animation. Yet now is time to assist our allied dog.

"We need to return the favor Forjah did for each of us regarding employment. He presented every skill and position in order to bring us up to speed. Now we need to instruct to him everything about being a gargoyle, the Vayl, and Taxonomy."

"He rejects everything including us. There is only harm in forcing further." Vision is first to jump to this most obvious and simple ended conclusion.

"Progression is vital." Losse contradicts. "Otherwise he is allowing the oppressor to win by allowing himself to be brought down." Before any of my crew members can grant an input, it is Commander Clevarest who brings forth.

"Without force or motive, expose him to everything! Show him your taxons, natures, perspectives, and especially the Vayl. Allow his mind to form its own inspiration, as gargoyles have always done."

SCENIC 20

I go over in my head the possibilities of my infection location, but amount only to overwhelmingly impossible odds. Clevarest indicates oyle effects all differently, some hours or days. The transmission must be physical, so it somehow interacted.

"What if I was gargoyle since birth, and just now surfacing?" I contradict against Jasmine's doubt.

"Does not work that way," Ares rules out while the three of us look out over the identical balcony still under repairs of the glass proposed as locoyle proof. He, despite the limited care of balance, perches on the railing with only one leg for support. I am finding myself comfortably positioned in the well-known gargoyle stance. Eerie as it is, natural as it feels.

"Out of our signature pose." Trident warns by resting chest over chin, and arms over his leg leaning over the banister. "Taking chances is what we don't by risk of exposure."

Transferring onto my hind legs, I then bring forth my next wonder.

"What is the point of gargoyles? They, we are just infused with the reptilian to make us fertile for reproductive purposes. To an extent, I feel pressured into taking advantage of being a species again; manifesting against my will."

"Like being forcefully infected."

"Exactly Ares, but why are you a gargoyle, why did you choose it?" The hagine shifts in his position the way his mind adjusts to my inquiry. With a breath signifying his preparation, he answers.

"Bios. She in a way, insisted every motive I went along with. Now I just make the best of it, cause even if the choice was mine, the result would be no different."

"He would still be the hyenine before us now. Partner and student. Yet Forjah, most of us know little about being dragon-mammals. We are humbly employed to stop locoyles, but whenever that is complete, how can we continue on?"

"It is not like we can blend into society. Once the eggs hatch and those goylings are ready to move on; they will not be able to incorporate. If other creatures see even one mammal younger than our generation, they will retaliate in ways unthinkable. Cause the only way for mammal offspring now is to be gargoyle." Despite being priorly unaware, Ares' strategic and wisdom branded mind has really put all into perspective.

"Too intense to process. Only adding to this overwhelming fire."

"You and your metaphors. At times they even stump me."

"Forjah has taken the multiple plates onto the single barbell." Trident echoes in his own figurative speech. "He will not be able to support it without us on each side. That is why we are going to introduce you deeper beyond the delve."

There is nothing I have to even balance his forceful offer.

For nothing feels right to me, nor does anything feel wrong. To progress is my one and only solution, wherever that may be.

"We will enter underground after our close. We will expand on the tour Dixon briefly granted to get you in tune. Let us teach you new facts and let your mind and instinct draw to what attracts."

"We know you desire to find your infection origin, and this is where you must begin. Educate yourself in as much info as possible and then work through the past to retrace where your hinds set."

Taken aback by the statement, I look to Trident in a brief awe.

"He is a Wise Ignoramus." I know the meaning of these two words, yet their combo.

"Is that a . . ."

"Oxymoron, yes. Every Gargoyle fashions a two termed contra; I am Thermal Icicle. You should independently form your own. Something to reflect you internally." Before having the chance of further informative, a group of geckos approaches the track, to which the three of us leap the balcony rail. One passing upon the concrete, we make way to the gate. This night I will return to the Delve, which is returning the identity of another to my thoughts. Hymnock, she is ever so desperate to assist as my guide. I know that I really need her.

"Ready when you are not." I declare in uncensored sarcasm. "Is the vault room our point of entry?" My chance of catching them off guard is quickly forgotten while Losse plays off my uneducated ignorance.

"You know that route. To closer approach our level, we will start with you picking a room here in the lodge." The retract of my head sets my neck in an upright position to bring my ears back in tandem with the response. Is she too being humored by sarcastically toying off me?

"Pick any one, withhold no curiosity," advises

Trident. Leaning on the wall before the doorway just beyond, Ares is giving an ear twitch in direction of the cellar. Let alone that would be my first choice regardless.

"The Cellar," I decide. We all cram in a nonlinear formation down the descending ramp into our low-level domain. Having no idea what will come next, Trident and Losse pull me to the center among the cushions while Ares sides with Jade and tigress and molly patiently hold back.

"Take a gander and study the structure." Losse obviously hints at something she holds strongly concealed behind her varg's muzzle. Vision is the last to join with her heavy set hinds beating the floorboards on impact.

"Having nothing better to occupy myself."

"Join us" offers Neon while vixen takes a stance behind the billiard table aside her.

"Fox," Trident exclaims in reclaiming my attention, "Observe the room and seek what stands out like a flower among weeds."

"Don't overthink," warns Jasmine, "keep in mind the first discovery you made leading to becoming gargoyle." With their advice passed, she and Trident take a position against the wall, leaving me the lone soul in the room's center. Looking from eye set to eye set, I find equal expressions of excitement that is most definitely building their suspense.

My first clue is that I know we are headed to the Delve; pairing that with my first finding. Now I am remembering to study the structure, like how my locker had the metal wall instead of the brick. Yes, an abnormality. So is that what I must seek?

Scanning up and down, I begin memorizing the symmetry of the room then I find a part not matching its reverse. In their right of the room at the furthest corner is a cylindrical pillar rotating to reveal our rack of pool cues, chalk, and replacement tips. But why build only one and off to the side?

Neon and Vision move aside in allowing my inspecting. Rotate it open to reveal the billiard gear as I know it. Upon completing the inspection, I instinctively step into the rotator just before the rack. Unsure whether they are observing or not, I slide the panel closed and am astounded the interior rotates in the opposite direction on hidden swivel. Turning me a full 180° before another very familiar tunnel into the dark underworld.

"Swell discovery." Losse praises by coming through on her own. She and I move ahead and allow the rest to pile in. Trident gives a praiseworthy slap over my back while Jade advises we do not use our voices in the underworld for fear of detection. When we are each accounted for, Losse takes the lead down into the Delve.

"Every room?" I exclaim in outpouring disbelief.

"Every room?" Jade repeats in only adding to the mystery flowing through my mentality. "Not a single one is prebuilt without an entrance or passage."

"Gargoyles are behind almost every business and organization." Jasmine joins in to unify the alluring conversation. "Construction especially, for we need it to construct a new tunnel entrance with every addition."

"Remember the history of the shoninki?" Neon recalls with her own inclusion. "The known and the unknown of their culture? Well, Taxonomists are the modern evolution." Now my brain is reaching its daily limit of what can be processed. "Yes, shinobi." The tigress synonymously details while comfortingly bringing her tail around over hind paws to perch upon the rock stump.

Not feeling near as uncomfortable as before, I attempt in holding ground over my own flat surfaced boulder in grand effort in concealing concern. Yet, I have far too much to even start feeling awkward.

"I really want to see Hymnock." I force out in attempt to further shield the arising nausea.

"She is here." Losse instigates the lone desire of my motive, "she has been waiting for your flee." Trident closes all my worry with the finality.

"There is no moving on for her. She now follows your lead."

"Even I have no idea where that is."

"She is near to raise you as her own, for you did not hatch from an egg. Rather, your mammalian hide."

Though I am putting nothing forth past muzzle, a thought is forming in my frontal lobe. Is she meant to be overseeing in a maternal sense?

Hoping to draw away from getting into the subject, I am now diving into another uproot. "Taxons, how do they work?"

"Hey Vision, you have been quiet the duration of time here. Why not have you explain it?" The zerda is in no high spirit as she looks up from her focused grip over the spring bar at his suggestion. It resembles a crutch, a deadly steel crutch.

Whether in approval of Trident, she instantly delves into taxonomic detail.

"The Taxons are Action, Combat, Strategy, Stealth, Adventure, Survival, Horror, Fantasy, Ethereal, and Sci-Fi. They are sort of like a classification of conducts for gargoyles. We each attribute our stratagem, gamut retainment, and role-play to the one best suiting our liking. Once becoming full fledged Taxonomist, it is then we learn tuning our taxon with the Vayl to achieve and express its impossibilities."

Taking in as much as possible from her description, I relate to her crowbar tool in my own pry for more detail of emphasizing.

". . . and the Vayl is?" Our newest crew member clutches close to her steel spine. Ares who is seated alongside the vixen, takes the reigns, to her relief.

"Everything. Mental, material, and mystical becomes a memory. We collectively define them as gamuts, as they are the range of memories. Yet every memory is not simply forgotten by every mind, it is rather collected in the ambient cache we refer to as the Vayl. A realm of deceased animas accessible only by Taxonomists."

"Wise Ignoramus." Losse repeats before going deeper into explanation, "Ares is a strategist taxonomist as it surely shows."

"But even an advanced mind such as my own cannot give the amount of what we already know of the Vayl."

"What we do know," Jasmine returns," is that it is unpredictable and always changing."

Jade then further kindles her description with, "it is either under one's control or completely out of it."

"A sort of behind the scenes structure." Neon proclaims, "one that balances our physical reality and all interactions. Everything from what each of our senses can interact with to what we cannot completely understand or even detect."

"Only accessible by reptiles and gargoyles," Trident defines by adding his layer of mystery, "the absolute best way to understand even the smallest portion of the Vayl, is to access it yourself."

SCENIC 21

The musk and early scent draws in my senses to an unexpected but welcomed extent. Even if I had never been raised in the rural earths and woodland, the dark secluded regions would swallow me without conflict. Even from my earliest days as a kit, all the bleak chilled atmospheres were counteracted by either a borderline forge fire or bodily closeness to substitute my yet to come manipulative body temp.

All the nights curled up in the quilts of cotton and wool, breath carrying out as the breath of the gargoyles wailed in the night seeking prey. Yet now in truth they were locoyle on the hunt, I even might call them prey of the true gargoyles.

The tunnel is now narrowing and sloping up into stone and earth corridors. The uneven carve and hollowing is ideal for grip and ascension, much like how it was described to me as an escape tunnel with many difficulties in navigation. Surely a gargoyle or locoyle would have a tough attempt at passing through.

When my leisurely approach to the surface is growing the most tiring, arrival of a strong fresh scent of night air filters down in taste tingling my tongue and nostrils. Then the announcement of crickets chirp unified with their fellow exoskeleton relatives as the finale of this ascending expedition. Fresh light reaches my pupils of the shimmering stone damp against my pads from the recent settle of dew.

"Lunar light . . ." Before I can complete the phrase of my own realization, that same heat I am learning beyond acceptance, returns from the tips of my paws as they have just reached out into the shimmering reflections of the white light. A yellow spark flares up upon a nail before many smaller ones ignite up as my hairs fold over and form into those crimson imbricates of my gargoyle hide. My grunts bellow out as I am compacted with garment trapped wings.

"Forjah," calls a voice only heard nights ago without trouble of identifying. Clearing the last of the tunnel, I am greeted by the humid breath of a great scaled snout before me. Hymnock allows me to grasp the horn nubs above her lips as I am heaved into the newborn night. After assisting my third set of limbs out from under my Escape uniform, she takes a position at my side as I begin taking in our vista.

Both urban and rural, the diurnal metallic towers spread out beyond the nocturnal trunks of green topped trees.

"Truly both sides of society." Hymnock confirms my observation. "You know both sides as I am informed, a frontier from the point of birth."

"Birth, yes. Not hatched, I am sure you fathom the meaning."

"The last generation, you and your colleagues. Sad to see no more mammals taking up education or even the birth rate. It really is over . . . "

"It is not of my concern, I want to continue devoid of any

inclusion over what cannot change."

"A long time it is, as now part reptile, your life is extended."

"Not to repopulate as the spiritual successor to mammals, that is just forcing me to use advantage of being a species"

"Then what is your motive of action? What is next for the gargoyle whom I swore to guide from before I heard your birthing roar?"

"I need you." I openly admit, "if you have options I desire to hear you out. My one impulse is to hunt my infector for passing their oyle into me."

"I nor any of our allies would even attempt at preventing you. Justice is the right course, but we feel fear that you would take out your infector beyond the fairness we accept."

"Your concern is that I may unleash wrath and threaten, if not take, their life. So what, nothing more than prey that deserves a mortal purpose."

"Purpose only to satisfy your revenge? That is deep coming from one so inexperienced."

"Now that I am gargoyle, why not use what they made me to teach them their dead place?"

"Do you really mean such claims, are you not still delusional from your shedding?"

"I know nothing more. This trial has betrayed me and severely challenged my morale."

"That is why I am here now at your side. To guide you through the transition."

"What if I was infected negatively, what if I am a locoyle?"

"Then you will be restrained in your mother's grip, locked behind the keratin of my claws."

"Exactly what . . . "

"Gargoyles view the dragons as mothers and fathers,

being it was us that saved your race and bring you to the halfway point between mammal and reptile."

"So metaphorically, I am your son?"

"If you reject that view, I will hold absolute respect. Just know that I am your transistor."

Now I am in no position to make any choices. The mental and physical fatigue grinds me dull and numb, but what if she is right, am I still in heavy influence of the oyle burning fresh between my mentality and physicality?

"Do you know the gamuts?" Hymnock challenges after I have comfortably positioned before the sky and tree line.

"Gamuts, the range of memories."

"Life force animation? Rendering? Rasterizing?"

"Is this vocabulary physically documented?" I scoff in disbelief.

"Absolutely. We believe in the parchment remembering instead of a cluttered mind. I am thankful Dixon and our colleagues have left much for me to pass on."

"Gamuts. Allow me to expand beyond the definition." Hymock repositions from her thick scaled legs to rest alongside with equal attention to the great silhouette of the skyline. The immense size of her tail mistakenly thrusts me to the cliff edge. In a retract of my esophagus, I force out in a gargled cling to the stone face.

"Example?"

"Literature, media, and almost every form of fiction. Gamuts are especially prevalent in youth, as they have a higher ratio of random process and greater cling to materialistic objects."

"All those stories I am exposed to, are actual?"

"Fictional for the majority, I assure you. Yet the power of gamuts manifests much to reality. At times it is even on a disturbing level, whether from history or fiction."

"Not sure I want all the details. I wish I was never

infected and continuing on with complete ignorance of all that is happening around me."

"Where would you be now if this had not occurred?"

"At rest for tomorrow, or up late playing Chimerical with my mates"

"Why this? Do you not even realize or acknowledge a reason you are here now?"

"Whatever that may be, I am here against my will."

"Why not use it? Don't let the enemy know you are here feeling hurt and violated. Do what they most certainly don't want and rid any control they are attempting."

"My desire is to hunt them."

"Your plan when you do?"

"All depends on my mood of that time."

"There is a violent savage in you. A vengeful one who will do all he can to prevent any from getting in his way."

"None manipulate me," I finalize.

"Pumera." The night is at a point I am no longer keeping track. Hymnock is at my side like a long lost ally, but every part of our relationship is freshly undeveloped. She has not given a vibe of either positive or negative; is this a sure sign she is pushing my will out progressively like the prick of her mighty horns?

As I am hurt and angered to a whole new extent, there is a deep plea in the depth of my mentality associating that I am not myself. Nor that my mind is clearly in sense. My instinctive desire to hunt my infector is strong just as she sensed. Yet is this rage new, or has it just been awaiting this moment to break free and unleash?

"You must visit her. She may not appear, as she chooses when to contact and not vice versa."

"Pumera?"

"Yes, the goddess of life force animation. Yet she is more than this simply assigned obligation. Come." The command is somewhere in a tone between a demand and pry. Yet I partially turn it down with an aching need to utilize my newborn limbs.

"A fine risk, for one so inexperienced gargoyle."

My reptilian companion remains alongside as I spread the third set and thrust off the cliffside the night atmosphere.

"Feel the updraft, the thermals, use those sails as your new set of arms." Despite losing my airborne in only a short duration, Hymnock agrees I have made progress.

"Like the newborn bovine, they learn quick on how to use their limbs." She swoops me up on her back before I draw close to an impactful landing. In our detour, we rise over the forested tree branches, ever closer to the cliffside just outside the fresh water shoreline. Only a cliff climb away from the sand, do we land atop its grass patch surface.

"Glide to the shoreline and call for her." Hymnock gives no other instruction, and I instinctively feel I should not make a request. Summoning my remaining confidence, I drop off the cliff side in sure clearance from the stone and earth wall. Membraned appendages locked open, I dive into a glide. Missing the point of the shoreline proves comforting to me as I become submerged in the shallows. To utilize the joint flex of the still foreign chiroptera tools is only quelled by the sensational chill counteracting their numbness.

SCENIC 22

Temperature is rarely at a level tolerable on either polar side. Basking in every amount of diurnal light, the heated concrete of the track both reflects and absorbs the thermal energy.

The Delve is much the opposite. Retaining my warm blood allows me to appreciate the chill here in the hollowed cavern. I never bothered asking Jasmine, or any poikilothermal how they keep a relative neutral temp. I know there is never a moment I come here without seeing one warming themselves before fire. Which also lead to my bring up of how the smoke exhausts from down under ground.

Neon explained our Delve was constructed deep below that foundry and oil refinery; to my astonishment of it being abandoned long before the last era. There is a great many system of piping stretching hollow from the high roof overhead and up into the deserted industrial area. With smoke and exhaust going almost the entire duration of night and day, it gives the illusion all is still functional.

We gargoyles require sleep minimally, as the reptilian form rests behind our hides daily and vice versa. The first time after my molting, I returned to my mammal form by mistake and awoke with a refresh almost delusional. Having two bodies that swap rest and function is greater than when I only had to deal with one.

Here I perch on a sitting rock in the shrouded cavern awaiting without out reason and only instruction. Dixon detailed I will be joined shortly. Knowing I cannot wait here long, my own Oyle is already burning hot. I still remember the night after of shedding, awakening in the chamber down in these cold depths. Only when Dixon witnessed my soundness, did he classify me as sane. Literally every time I transition between bodies, the oyle demands movement, and now this morning I am getting dangerously close personal tolerability.

Deciding to distract my mind in observation, I take in the active life of the Delve. As I and my colleagues reside up top at the Escape lodge, there are entire kin of hatchlings, rookery's where parents never leave eggs unattended, various dealers of what cannot be acquired on the surface, and an astonishing amount of Taxonomy.

Yet here or at the lodge, I do the very minimum of tasks at paw, not taking advantage of anything the escapists rave about.

I was not born in to this life, nor is it of my choosing. I am first and still the lone enforced by oyle. Now capable of flight thanks to a new pair of limbs, no longer needing to sleep, and rejuvenated reproduction; none peak any amount of interest.

Break of will is a sort of grounding grudge and weight upon flight enabled sails. The instinctive drive is to vengefully hunt my infector. None here or up-top support my retaliation, yet none have opposed it. Hymnock, my guide, supported my elected testing for delayed inheritance and accidental infection.

Yet everyone confirmed it external, by force of will.

As I look upon the lives of the inhabitance of mammal or gargoyle, I ready for any suspicious glares. Every moment here, I think what if my infector is among them hiding from view. Sighting past the first layer, the second, the following, I land upon one pair of irises capturing my gaze rather than vice versa.

I know of him from legacy and verbal of muzzle. Though it is a warm season and he is of short leathery antlers, it is no doubt the same with that dark determined glare.

Jasmine, a well-respected gargoyle currently in his buck form of virginianus. Why is am I receiving his attention, why is he breaking through the crowds directly before me. His mighty cloven hooves only make the slightest click tapping over the cave floor surface. A control of footfalls I greatly admire from my traceur perspective Right as he clears the distance between us, the cervidae towers over baring a small pack of nylon.

"Forjah?" he greets. I have no auditory response and only layback my ears in a calm but blatant lack of understanding.

"You have successfully pronounced my moniker."

"Employed by Cleverast, known as your sire's offspring and the first enforced by oyle."

"You are really destroying my joy ignorance here." I impertinently criticize.

"Jasmine is what you will know me by. I know you are a dog of action rather than chat." In his own total ignorance to my attitude, he tosses the nylon pack where I receive it in my paws in instantaneous reflex. A hydro pack.

"I want that water drained by the time we are finished."

There is much desire to inquire where our destination is and why so, yet I recede as an inquirer to remain an actor. I have never been a one to follow a directive array of actions, rather just be surprised and reactively take on what manifests. Finding it one of the remaining joys still retained from my mammalia.

Jasmine leads to part of the underworld unfamiliar to me, a passage positions right above at the top of the tree root just beneath the ceiling. Where the highest pipes are visible for the swiftness of smoke. At its summit on the very end where the ancient shinobi ceased digging the Delve and only continued by the expanse of the tunnel between here and the surface.

"This is a first for me. Do I dare request the destination?"

"Ruins long abandoned, yet there is an ever growing reason for us to exist on. I pray one day for return to the surface when domestic finally understands we are the not enemy."

"I am in greater in hope for a cure to infertility, or a hybrid reversion."

"Your optimistic Forjah, that I admire and will build off." A grunt narrowly escapes into reverberation of my throat. Whether he acknowledged my disgust, the buck takes lead headfirst up the darkened spiraling tunnel.

Now a good three stories up, the fresh air reaching my cardio in a welcoming reception. The temp even rising as does my own in welcoming rise of the new day.

"Feeling refreshing sanity, Forjah?"

"The endorphins prove satisfying."

"You will be working up a heat, that I promise." Upon the inhaling clarity of the morning oxygen, light finally reaches our nocturnal eyes to signal our surfacing.

Stepping out to the near blinding light of the rising disc, I join Jasmine on a steel grate with its metallic grip touching the metatarsals of my hinds; astounded by every shimmer of the rusted cylinders.

"The refinery welcomes us in its corroded glory," greets Jasmine. A deserted ruin of urban steel and stone. Everything from the layers of great platforms, antenna towers and the same cylindrical towers venting out the same exhaustion from below. Though it is an abandoned place of rust and ware, I cannot fight the extreme urge breaking any form of dormancy. I am not taking in a marvel of architecture to serve energetic needs. I am observing an urban jungle of cement and urbex demanding metallics.

"Tell me Forjah, of the any benefits of being a gargoyle. What is the attribute that most pleases you?

"The duration since infection has proven nothing." Admittance is no form of conclusion leaping. When is honesty ever pain inducing?

"What is you do Forjah?"

"I am a go kart operator." The buck heaves a great breath before pressuring further. Where is he going with this?

"Dog, what is it you really do? I have been informed of your specific skill. You do it most often and even earned the nickname "ninja'; in favor of relation to our taxonomic predecessors."

Before I can eve decide a proper furthering for explanation, her concludes independently.

"I know you are a traceur, Forjah. For the exact amount you delve in, I can admire a humble individual keeping his skills tame."

"I do it to experience less like an urban a grounded dog. I am a beast and one with my environment."

"Show me," he requests.

"You want an entertaining experience? Why not hide in a cinema?"

"You are the real thing with potential to apply this to the gargoyle life."

"You want me to trace and entertain hybrids? Are go karts and batting cages not enough?"

"You are missing the point in its entirety, you are capable of applying these skills to aid in our gargoyle quest. Just process and expand your imagination."

"My one quest as you refer to it, is to find my infector."

"What will you do once you discover them?"

"Beat them, knock out their jaws. Show enforced wrath."

"Why not build your already acquired traceur strength? You have illusive potential for stealth taxonomy. I hate to pass on this fact, but you need to learn by adapting with what you have been dealt. As a member of vulpes, the creatures of adaptability."

"Come," he directs up a spiraling stair, "Race me to the top by your own rout." As long as I have been doing the art of displacement, I am much more at comfort in the places to where I began. Though I remember the advice of a most prominent figure . . .

"The way of the parkour is to continue, not to stay here" . . . now is not the time to contemplate, only act.

Before me, situates the catwalk tower encased by external framework resembling scaffolding. Rusted with loose bolts an uninviting surfaces, yet plenty of metal for assisted grip. Judging the first beam, I run forward in biped, pick up my strides, to then transition into a leap in a wall run. The black of my paw pad creates friction in a vertical step that I kick off to latch the first beam. The top out is the most difficult action that I have only mastered to a limited level. Once in a comparable balance on the first set, I seek out what next to displace too. I find my target, the exact support beam stretching from the silo to the catwalk tower. Doing all I can to avoid time loss, I top out again right below a pipeline slick with dried oil. This results in a soil to the skin beneath the fur, yet none of this holds back my greased digits.

The structure scaffoldings are closer in between, providing access of ease compared to what I just passed through. My fluency increases as I counteract any thought or urge to focus anywhere but up. The dome top of the silo in my reach presents an edge probable with plenty of grip for a good top out to surface. In a confident striding distance, I back up to the start point. Using gravity that is present, I accelerate forward to the launch in capability. Hinds reach the railing just before I grip over top with forepaws. The landing impact is by far a failure with the hard hit and vibration hitting every connected metal piece in the tower.

"Exceptional Forjah, I am positive you exceeded even your expectations."

"It's a failure." I point out, "You beat me up."

"An intentional misconception. I deceived you, as the purpose was to test your creativity. You thought differently about it despite my original challenge."

"There is extensive uniqueness to the thrill. The art of displacement is my one way of expressing physically." Taking a swig of the hydro pack, I am tempted is using it for oil cleansing, but that would present a cheat to the request of Jasmine.

"Take caution in the grease present. I am quite positive you are new to the obstacle."

"Far worse than a rainfall."

"This way," the buck directs, "deeper into the refinery where the petroleum hazard lessens." The catwalk leads two a towering maze of various platforms of a great variety and build.

"Is there any location here inaccessible?

"Maintenance was the architectural goal, but this also benefits us. You show me your push of capabilities while I observe and apply your skillset to taxonomy." Once in almost the exact center we arrive beneath the mammoth smoke tower, filtering the Delve arising from its innards.

"You ever flip?"

"Not efficient nor to my liking. Not a traceur's move. I have always seen it as a push of limits from getting to point one to point two. Flipping is for style and not progression. I have yet to be proven wrong."

"Locoyles won't be impressed, that is a definite."

The central tower is of such immensity that the platforms

surrounding it are of permanent build to the extent I cannot hear a single creak under my digits or Jasmine's ungulates. Here the scent of deep earthly smoke is strong yet weirdly refreshing in the cool air. Here presents the greatest view of the area, more towers of steel all connected by geometrically traveling pipes, forming their own grid layout around the refinery. There may be an extensive amount of glass shards and oil blotches, but it adds to the mystified reality of these ruins. Is it a paradox of a calming sadness to what is left behind, or am I thankful to its abandonment for a whole new location to explore?

Beneath the behemoth of the central hallowed tower, I am taking in the electrical tower that encases it like and exoskeleton. From our gradual ascent, my tongue salivates as more is revealed far below. The pipes, catwalks, platforms, and whatever every other metal contraption becomes a new form of obstacle in my head. When I had first began tracing, it was instructed that I would see all environments indefinitely different. Like the impossibility of reading an advertisement, my mind studies objects as obstacles with prep and planning just how to traverse it. This refinery in ruin presents possibilities far beyond that of lively domestic. Passed the stack and atop of the exoskeleton, I express to Jasmine my exact reaction of the urban jungle's call.

"I cannot claim to have doubted you, as I did not have it to begin with. Yet I am supercharged with traversing inspiration."

"You need a training ground to further your skills I assure can benefit. In the scale of night and hide by day, this region is at your disposal."

This hunger that has not overtaken me since discovering those marble walls aptly named cat-city. In the form of an uncontrollable urge to move and ascend over the platforms and every object in the environment.

Without warming, I push off the rusted metal grate to sail over the railing in gravitating below. Impacting on the balls of my hinds to a strong beam below. Assuredly positioning weight on the inside of my pads.

"You know much about not holding back." Jasmine comments landing beside me in clanging to the metal. Maintaining form to keep myself centered and balanced, I extend my tail as counter weight before explaining.

"Most danger arrives in the discipline from holding back. I have over shot obstacles, especially in my early training without injury; only to harm myself from hesitation."

"Just as you and I preform now." He gestures with a sight to beam over the peak, "balance is important." With this in mind's recollection, I move steady throughout the areas rooftops with minimal slowing and increased speed. Only a number of railings are loose with ware while the rest provide strong landing points. This only presents I have much to learn and perfect involving bars.

Jasmine points out the areas soiled in patrolmen, where I do my best in keeping them evasively in mind.

In an expanse of time untracked, the hydro pack is dry with only the last few drops in the hose. At location toward the most rundown sector, the remains of a brick building lay in barley a frame of an exterior. Testing its sturdiness, I'll teach Jasmine.

SCENIC 23

Time is an illusive way to track events when they happened and before those yet to come. The devotion I have given to waiting keeps me going by the fact I will succeed as I began long ago. It is not the individuals I see alone, but their mentalities of cynical loss. As though I could physically taste their processing as my exact thirst of appetite.

In the late night of my body feeling worn and faded from time, I cannot help but feel lost equally as before. My thick reptile hide is only counteracted by the warmth of the mammal body beneath. The pain of my mind interacts with all physiology, combatted only by inhalations of oxygen restoration.

Here I ponder the health we struggle to maintain along with the goals of my life and those personal to my students. Now I am struggling to keep enough air as there is little here in the earth. The only solace being who I will have under my instruction.

"Ethake." The voice of Raquel interrupts the night astoundingly devoid of locoyles. My pupil joins me, garbed in his own chestnut imbrications reminiscent of his desert decent.

"What troubles you, my inspirer?" Intaking another breath to prepare a proper response, I comfort him with a dual pawed massage over his worn wingless shoulder.

"I want to relieve the three of you, though it is taking longer than anticipated."

"Then blame us," he pleads. "We cannot compare and are slowing you down."

"Do not feel so guilty. If each of you were transitioned by now, the fourth would be all alone is his separation."

"You mean . . ."

"Yes, he has come to Delve. I need you, Marz, and Kodyk to retrieve him. For he wants exactly the same.

"As you command, my Queen." Intriguing how they refer to me. A moniker I had not requested but willfully accepted.

Few remember, as little has been documented. Taxonomists were not only preceded by reptiles in the ways of gamuts, for it was the shinobi who eventually evolved through the Taxons once becoming more familiar with the Vayl. As that is a time long before now, we gargoyles are not much more knowledgeable than the first. So little has been gained to the point of rumor or conspiracy. Even the mighty reptiles and presages will never wholly understand the Vayl. Yet if that is to happen, where would the thrill of the mystery be?

Kodyk is leading the route to the Delve that only his lupine mind has mastered in memorization. His granite scaled hide is a cold spot by his internal blood as he halts before the pond over a boulder casting its lunar shadow down under the shallows. Diving with wings limp and trailing behind his tail, the gargoyle disappears in submergence. Marz is next before I bring up the tail. If not for knowing her mammal side, I would not have guessed there is an aliurus beneath the stripes and teardrop hide of scales. She instead goes feet first and I dive to join the two in the chase for our new companion.

Now on the vayl side, we have arrived in the ambiance we know as the inbred wood. Trees of ancient times long dead and standing in our realm have overlapped by growing inside one another. Up to four types of monstrous trunks twisted into one to the point of dead leaves and fresh fruit sharing a branch.

Once we have cleared into the underground cavern, our oyle is burning cold and warm. The familiar earthly aroma of too many scents to count returns and makes us realize it has been long since our last encounter. Though we cannot get a near level training as our Queen provides; it is time to seek out our new partner.

Forjah-

Dawn is not far off for delivering the new day, for this night is expanding my knowledge of the Delve's layout. The great root is reserved as the rookery dens; with the nesting carveouts positioned from high to low. Beneath the gargantuan organic tower is that same shaft filtering light of night at day deep allowing for quick conversion. Just before the ray, is fire lit dome matching with the crater like interior dug beneath. Losse explains is the ancient record of the past shinobi and taxonomists long before they realized all could be recorded in the Vayl and its recalls.

"Quite little there that could be gained new. Yet does serve as where taxonomy began." Trident optimistically presents.

"So the records there are not recalls?"

"Few are," describes Jasmine, "but the modern recalls are far superior in number and quality."

"Efficient in both time and authenticity," Ares expands.

Jade superiorly projects "The first were literally doing double the work, and we are thankful to have learned from the past mistakes."

"Not to say we are not making any new mistakes ourselves."

"Ares has a point," Neon warns before leading into the record carve, "but we have the Presages."

"Presages, I have heard that title mentioned amongst us."

The crew begins withdrawing rolls and sheets to give me an example of how the first taxonomists thought and philosophized. But with the overload of info taking in, I have been pulling on the horns of my ears just trying to process the basics. Then asking the same question again gets them into a more stable level.

"The Presages," Ares praises in obvious admiration by a newfound glint contrasting the rest of his body, "are not yet ready to meet you."

"More so vice versa," inputs Losse while she organizes the sheets she had withdrawn from the clay storage platform.

"He does not even have a gauntlink." Jade's output has no effect on me, but I see the wide eyes of all here around.

"Now that, he is ready for!" Trident confidently expresses with a slam of his fisted reptile paw. None interject in directing us out, including I for lacking what a gauntlink is.

Whisked away through the center of the Delve, I am led past the food tents and into an internal part I am all too unfamiliar with. Just as we depart from the encampment, my eyes catch a familiar light; yet unfamiliar to the rest of the delve. Artificial lighting lines what is a carved tubular tunnel angling into the wall face. Aside this entrance are wooded troughs containing various ages and styles of metallic objects. Ignoring the assortments, I continue following through with the urban aroma of grease, fuel, and iron.

The corridor is significantly warmer with the artificial light, even sending a quite welcoming shudder. Passing carves along the sides, the first present are dark with no artificial other than the metallic scent of new and fresh metals. Yet activity begins to stir as we round a spiral stair in the corridor center forward into what I assume is the end with obvious change in more modern white lighting.

Passing under the ring-like carve, the temperature changes again like stepping out from a cold shadow. Presented in the cavern is a polished stone floor a far cry from the rest of the delve. Before us is stainless bar of steel lined with an unkept supply of devices I have no idea of how to identify.

Seated on a warn wooden barstool is a fossa, obviously outside her gargoyle form. With the exception of what look like small tusks protruding from either corners of her commissures, like a pair of horizontal teeth. Back at the Vayl point of Aise Shima, Ares elaborated that the Vayl can overlap and rupture even the physiology of a gargoyle. So my strategic assumption is that her gargoyle body is overlapping here in our reality.

"Jenuine, guess who is finally here." Trident presents in what I feel is a quite discreet way, while also motivating my independent introduction. The feline like creature looks up from her work of device disassembly the moment Neon steps out of view.

"The progeny of Sy," she declares with a click of those tusks almost worthy of an ASMR.

"I must convey your appearance inherits more from your dam."

"Well observed," I praise, "yet she and I only share a descent tree."

"Then I suppose," the female clears her voice by retracting her tusks, "you are Introspective?"

"Greater than likely." Ares assertively coins in to my complete misunderstanding. "Forjah has a while before he understands the perspectives; having only been a gargoyle for a number of days."

"Understandable. Despite you being the first from force, be thankful you were not in my position."

I feel like questioning this, though she immediately jumps ahead with, "I began as a Locoyle." A shudder trails over my new appendages in a numbness causing a disembodied feeling.

"He," Trident interjects a break of semi paralysis, "exhausted a locoyle on the first encounter." Though I am neutral toward that success, I have a sudden acquiring need to learn more from Jenuine.

"How long have you been a gargoyle?"

"I have been a true gargoyle since before you, the final generation was born. I was exhausted, rehabilitated, and introduced to chasing down the those neglectful of their own oyle. I prefer to see Locoyles as victims and not villains, they just need the help that I fortunately received."

"He is also a traceur," Jade points out against my own will, "he could become an exhauster almost flawlessly."

Jenuine bows and puts down the device along with the drive. "Then before that, you will need a gauntlink. To earn one you need to work very hard."

"He just may be an exception," Ares puts forth, "he did not choose nor inherit the life in the delve."

"True, yet that is up to Dyxon, and even the Presages. Until approval I cannot do much."

"Other than a rundown of how it works in your own linguistic," Jasmine forms indirectly.

"Your timing could not be better." Jenuine praises in monotone I respect. She beckons me forward with a point of claw over the device she had been disassembling. I cannot see more than an obvious exposed circuit board and metal plates that had a been the bezel and surfacing.

"How much of an explanation have you had of the gauntlink?"

"None." I admit in that same reptilian voice that continues feeling alien. Retreating behind the bar and pulling open a number of drawers, she returns with a bundle of various items held close to her breast before letting them drop in a pile.

"So the basic definition of the gauntlink is the triad of not only technology," she addresses again to the electronic components, "but also of biology and supernatural."

Following her so far, she presses on by picking up a single optical disc with a number of streaks from wear. Then holding out her right wrist, she presents a deep blue garb that wraps the top of her wrist and back of the paw. It is a comet like shape with the disc portion set upon her opisthenard and tail end contouring her wrist.

"Is that, bound to you?"

"As I said," the fossa repeats, "the gauntlink is tri-functional. Ever wonder why your crew always covered their fore arms in sleeves and gloves?" For a confirm, I look to my colleagues the moment they pull up and remove gloves to expose a monochrome of identical devices.

"These are gauntlinks," rephrases Jenunine,"and to reduce your lack of ignorance, they are only for us gargoyles as they are powered by our own oyle. The same that made us part reptile." To gain a proper vantage point, I kong vault upon the steel surface for a detailed visual; to which Jenuine nods that I am in fact a traceur.

Raising her gauntlink to me, she places the edge of the disc just above it while explaining that it is a recall. Placing the tip just below her knuckles, it then disappears by feed. She then picks up a few slate colored chips and holds them in a stack; doing the same by inserting them into the tip. Yet, they do not feed but rather oscillate around the disc, plausibly on a belt or chain, loading one by one into the side of the tail of the wrist mount.

"You, are putting them in your body?"

"Oh I am sure she has accepted worse things inside."

142

I bark in the deep vocals toward my colleague in utter disrespect, but Losse seems far darker in mood, gloating over the loose gauntlinks stacked before Jenuine. Her tone was almost forceful against her current feelings, yet Jenuine ignorantly goes on detailing.

"The recalls are actually entering the vayl, through my gauntlink, empowered by the oyle of my body." Not in need of understanding her explanation, this perfectly makes the device a triad of the technological by the hardware of the gauntlink itself, the oyle of her biology being its power source, and somehow supernaturally linking ultimately to the vayl.

Now Jenuine exposes a plastic casing with an obvious chip teeth exposed at the bottom. She then plops it down directly over the arch top of the tail, where two bay doors open and accept the cartridge inside before closing. Proceeding to explain it, too, is a recall of an older but still reliable model.

"These are three recalls of the most common type, as such they are disposable and capable of reformation."

"Yet they are called recalls for the sake of recording gamuts from the past?"

"Not only a record taker but a reminiscence simulator." She then persuades me in watching her eyes closely in demonstration. The first obvious change appears in her corneas as they begin fading before going to tint, and finally an illuminating white like a pair of organic torches.

"I am witnessing the memory stored in this recall visually." Jenuine conveys by staring off in the distance absorbed in her own reality," my eyes are oyle filled right now with the gauntlink projecting the recall's gamuts directly over the liquid of my pupils, granting an introspective experience of the taxonomist. This is only entering the Vayl's stored memory through a window, and one can even take it further by entering the memory fully.

"Like how we did in Aise Shima," Ares elaborates in a

reliving point of converged understanding.

As blunt as I am with consistent praise, the reason is that I can rarely put gratitude into a verbal level. This form of awestruck is no different now as I am taking in and properly absorbing these marvels. As gargoyles, we can use our oyle not only as an energy but also a direct link to the cache of memories. But the fact that it submerges inside our eyeballs to project the collected memories of taxonomists . . . this may take a time unpredicted to fully capture.

For a new witness of comparison, Trident approaches and withdrawals his own gauntlink with a swivel of chips oscillating around the disk into a fan blade configuration. Jenuine withdraws her own chips, yet they form a more feminine paper fan configuration . . .

"Ohh! its gender specific?"

"Right On!" They praise.

"Understand. Everything physical, mental, and spiritual is measured in gamuts which feed into the archive we know as the vayl. The memories created and unintentionally recorded are that of personal Anima, which becomes an Ambiance in the Vayl after death." Jenuine glances toward Ethelwulf who is still sloped over the stacked gauntlinks like a looming varg observing her cubs defensively. Only does the inclusion of her explanation converge exactly what Losse is experiencing.

"These are the gauntlinks of those we have lost. I hate allowing abandoned items to waste," she implies with a neutral tone balancing out their lost and found.

"So many," our lone lupine exasperates, "we gargoyles are few enough even before our birth as the final generation." I am in direct position here not knowing a way to console her, for the lost taxonomists I will never know. Though I am unsure who has perished at the cost of the Locoyles, could taxonomists not make up for it by rehabilitating locoyles as they have obligated to?

Thanking Jenuine, we depart from the assembly cavern with a contagious tranquility set over us by the amount of casualties. I am among the few to have lost allies especially at the immature state of life, yet I want to live as much as they wanted to perish.

"Why am I remaining?"

Everything I have gained tonight is worthy of filling a notebook. Yet even that would be a fraction of the world occupied by gargoyles and Taxonomists. Unlike the opposing domestic world, there is no single record of how everything works; on the cause that nothing here and in the Vayl is certain. There is more that we do not understand and much of it may never change. It is up to each of us individuals to learn and discover through experiences and study of the vayl. Being fond of the so called presages, Ares explains, "Presages are the prospective taxonomists with unlimited connection to the unknown. Though devoid of emotion and philosophically apathetic, they do have morals and see a right and wrong. However, an overwhelming amount of external gamuts can give them a sort of false personality. The fine example of going too far, is the awol psychotic presage, Hekate."

I could question why I was unlawfully infected and the overall purpose accumulated from it overall. Though, I can do nothing to change this occurrence; so there is nothing to gain from criticism. Waste of word is pointless as always.

Here in the night over the oil refinery where Jasm granted motivation, I trace to get a better grip on my new body. As different as it is to displace in a reptilian body, the greatest nuisance is the two extra appendages attached against the same shoulders supporting my forearms. Much like an awkward double joint, locking them against my backbones does not help. All I can do now is await the dawn light to bask my scales and return the fur hide.

The black of my immature coat lightened out as I

biologically progressed. With carful focus and precision, I free solo the abandoned oil silo slower than I am capable of as a vulpine. Before, I assured scales were hard, especially that of dragons. Yet my scales don't feel all that strong compared to the flesh and fur of my mammal body. Overall, the sensation presents as my hairs flattening out into the crimson imbrications that are. Stroking them in reverse even simulates their tender growth, while the horns in place of my vulpes ears are ridged in hard layered keratin. Being I am still a newborn, will my scales harden along with the horns? Which even feel loose like the antler of a cervidae. Assuredly, the amount of development my body had cannot compare to the life of learning before me in and outside the Vayl.

As dawn approaches, I feel the same energy depleting as it would from a long day at the track. I do not have sleep to look forward to as my body will revert back to mammal and be completely refreshed. Ready for the surface life as a go kart operator.

Mind carries on the emotional stress weighing me down to bring my body at rest against fighting the will. Yet this may be the one escape from it all.

"Dog." A barbed scale foot prods my side. Succeeding my ears, I feel my lungs enrich the air as I force eyes open and find myself upon the silo with dawn light now shimmering off the remaining rusted silver.

"Haven't seen a gargoyle sleep in a great amount of time," a female voice observes. Returning upon haunches in the gargoyle squat, I find three new hybrids circling me in choreographed sync. The males are obviously canine in appearance while female looks Procyon, or even Ailuridae.

"He's a newborn, still grasping this new reality."

Against their own expectation, I gander on them silently awaiting their introduction, before catching on that they technically are the intruders.

"I am Raquel," the warm chestnut male addresses. "This is Kodyk, and Marz," he then finalizes.

"Forjah," I return. "Am I trespassing?"

"In truth, each of us are," Marz brings up, "yet this meeting is not a random encounter."

"We would like to transport you to our queen." Kodyk jumps in ahead of any description, "you desire what we do and she offers it."

"The fact of your violation makes you a perfect candidate," Marz adds in perfect sync to finish his declaration.

"Dog, being you have been forced into this and are pressured with what you don't want, the best answer is our inspirer. Because of her animation, she sensed us as she did you."

"What does she want?" I demand in dazed bliss.

"It is not only what she wants," Marz stimulates in an alluring disembodied tone. "It is what you want, dog."

SCENIC 24

This area is much like the delve in both visual and nasal sensory. Though it does not provide explanation to why it feels removed.

I recollect to when I was a kit, living in the frontier at the time when sire and dame lived. So many sights my eye recorded that my body could never experience in the early days as an AOD. When my ankles and hind pads were only beginning to condition, I could never go far beyond the territory when dawn came near. Why then am I ascending through this sloping cave mouth with three new gargoyles in the drape of night? Having not had as much of a rustle from predatory assault?

All distraction overtakes my realization at the peak I have known since kit hood, yet only a distant sight back then. I had visualized climbing it, seeking a potential tracing spot; but always held back by what I continue to misunderstand.

To an incredible surprise, once the darkness is at max, my eyes begin adjusting as the temp picks up to a looming warmth almost like a thermal imaging cam. Yet the light only escapes momentarily before it returns on shimmer against carved stone.

I have been led into a chamber with a single ray of light raying down from an inlet toward the looming stalagmites. To where the stars of night silhouette a single figure posed contemplating on supporting hinds.

"Queen, he has accompanied us," Marz voices out in a projected echo. The individual shifts her neck to reveal predatory illuminated eyes that I and many carnivores possess. Yet I am disproven when she drops to our level in revealing she is indeed gargoyle with a toned body showing age and experience.

"Forjah. Like the ears of your responder, Hymnock. I have heard your birthing roar against the force that dragged you in against contradicting will."

The female approaches calmly with paws near silent that I respect as a traceur. She stands a head higher than I and just below the ear points of Kodyk. A powerfully robust jaw spreads to present a thick toothed build reminiscent of a reptile's. Duo with a pair of soft eyes reflecting the oyle filled scleras and corneas. Contrasting her scaleless amphibious hide, I cannot simply bypass the rising palpitation in my breast. Is my natural attraction finally setting into my hybrid body?

At instinct far ahead of my control, my paw raises at mid joint following my shoulder. It comes to rest in the cold cradle of her own, assuredly feeling irradiated. Yet as the night before contrastingly grew brighter, I find all sight darkening the image of my digits resting in her metacarpal. My eyes suddenly feel weighted and even hurt to the point where I am holding my head in its building migraine.

Growls form in the voice I am still growing accustomed to. While I almost fall to my knees in this strikingly negative bliss. The great paws of Kodyk grasp me in support, but it is the cold digital pads of the Queen that rest over my scalp in her beckoning to withdraw my lids. Opening, I find my sight returned with her directly overhead in cradling my head just below the horns.

"First time your eyes filled with Oyle, I assume." She describes in the enticing relief beyond my expectation, "it occurs frequently before you gain physical control. That is why I am volunteering assistance in your development. But especially, your ultimate desire."

Rising up with the help of her pupils, I know somehow; she is more aware than anyone of my long progressing need. For the first time, I almost let it slip from my tongue . . .

As the light approaches, so does the new day. Ares and I are setting the last of the salvage engines to rest on the ever increasing supply shelves.

"Can't go out yet, not until light." I agree with him, though I would rather wait until it passes its rays down through the cupola, despite it taking longer and would waste time.

"Where is Forjah, why miss an opening morning?"

"With the change of his physiology, mind, and spirit, he himself is personally changing."

"Yet more distance and seclusion cannot be an answer. Involvement is the one way to learn."

Ares raises a paw in a calming action before presenting,

"First he must find himself in order to place inside our underworld."

Though I am credited for upbringing Ares to the level he is in now, he is already becoming an independent hagine closely comparative to the rest of our crew. Positively, his animation has allowed our diverse personalities to influence and affect him while he looks past our negatives and does not judge. Yet I cannot shake the concern he may be getting Forjah wrong.

While the hagine tracks a list of our parts on order, I prepare the proper tools for my continued rebuilding of the #VII cart; directly beneath the cupola soon to ray down and deliver us into mammalia.

Taking note of what I have recorded in my gauntlink, I am able to salvage a good amount from the recalls in the vayl, granting a balance of budget. Yet it will not last and soon no memory of these inanimate machines will be left as the memory cache changes indefinitely. We are not so different as the last generation.

"Losse is approaching," Ares calls out in the dark. I expect to hear her pads over the concrete, but she rather materializes from the darkness of the shadows here in the garage. I hug the varg before I can get too soiled in engine grease. Even before Ares has the chance to point it out, I sense her mind is not at ease.

"Statistically," Losse exhales on carnivorous breath, "with the lack of locoyles; everything feels like the calmness before the storm. I even heard some domestic rumor they are gone for good. The only solace I found this night, is watching over to catch and observe for distress of any prey."

"It is not right," Ares ratifies by closing up a manual, "and those out and about also include Forjah."

"None of us can be alone anymore." I declare, "we may be healthy dragon mammals, but even we have limits. Dyxon has not made a statement, but we must begin watch shifts at night. Everyone will take shifts like we do here at every event point."

"Leave it all to you Ares," the varg comments, "thinking at a level close to the Presages themselves."

"Observed," I soulfully palpitate, "the time for us to be still as statues above the light pollution has arrived. Yet we cannot force our newest recruit right away, he has had far too great an extent lately."

'We have extended lives," Losse reinvigorates, "our times of freedom will be rare yet all the more special."

Her inclusion is even further emphasized by Ares' addition of, "optimistically, we are doing this for the future hatchlings."

Like the intention to cut off his declaration forces our attention to divert, it is not night nearing its end with first light beginning to peak the horizon. The form it takes is a spontaneous yet welcoming silhouette fluttering down. A figure of extreme petiteness with what appears to be a long slender straw like appendage protruding at head mount.

"Quite early for an Avian, huh Snowdrop?" Losse suggests to the opposing female. The hummingbird comes to rest over my shoulder before implying.

"Too much of nothing going on," she reflects on our current subject. "You gargoyles are immature to a level, yet admirably adapt when you know it is of the greatest need."

"That is accurate," our hagine escapist details in a monotone phraseology, "and our need now is to find our lost crew member."

"Oh?" The trochilidae hen voices out amongst the hums of her wings with the faintest hint of sarcasm. "Is it a certain dog go kart operator who intentionally gets lost?"

"The one and only," we confirm.

"There will be a fresh selection of maple when you find him," Losse promises between varg and hen.

"It is just, locoyles will not prey on the diminutive plumage of an avian."

She flutters her wings to illusively show her snowflake display before taking off into the dawn with, "'Not like I would refuse otherwise."

Average avians out here are limited in sensory, yet despite not being mammal reptile or even gargoyle, Pumera herself granted me a personal animation. At first I was only paired with Trident before warming up to the remainder of the crew; metaphorically against the algid nature I share with him and Jasmine. Yet like the taxonomists, I too lack a full understanding of my abilities. Only recently finding I do not attract locoyles with my blood nor the defining sound of my wings. Presenting an invisible sensation to the creatures, whether it be my furtiveness or their complete ignorance.

As for the feline like dog I seek, I know him the least of the crew. Despite being the first among Escape and a dear companion to my companions; he is a big introvert and quite distant even amongst a crowd. Yet as Losse feared and Ares predicted, being alone amongst suspicious tranquility is a deep risk. Especially for the newborn dragon mammal Forjah is.

As for locating him, I flutter into the chilled air high above the trees and look out over the wild where I know he originates and dwells in isolation from the domestic. Knowing he is of homeothermic oyle makes it rather easy to start, as I sense a warm body far out in direction of a granite peak. The thermal aura acts like a bullseye against its surroundings. A homing signal standing out against the approaching dawn.

For the first time, I am feeling an emotional ease in this new body. Here with Ethake and her students, this new calmness eases my cardio like the first breath following birth. The light is almost here and my fur will return as I will to escape. Raising head up with muzzle pointed, I voice out, "May I return, Ethake?"

"I am here for you, when you are ready," she obliges with an overlap of her amphibious digits. "Even when you cannot sense it."

My head falls at a bow of my neck the moment tears begin falling from my dilated pupils. Running black to temporarily blind in my own oyle, I collapse at risk of losing consciousness.

Only where she is here to catch me mid descent with receiving paws and outpouring voice, "you are about to be refreshed, Forjah. Return at night when you see fit; here I will remain and here you will find us."

"Thank you . . ." is all I can bring up in gratification. As I turn tail, the light touches to the feeling of scales overlapping away to the warmth of fur. Shedding over in replenishment as I return to quadruped and make my way out into the dawn. Feeling not only physically refreshed but spiritually as well. This sheltered sensation has not been present since before my dame and sire perished so long ago.

After clearing the mist and dipping below the trees, I surprise the dog by a descending flutter causing him to retract in quadruped.

"Four legs, still defensive as ever." Being he is in mammal form, he must have caught the first rays of day to be reverted by now.

"Snowdrop!" He exclaims in a bark that rings with his new set of reptile vocal cords.

"The one and only," I retort, "finding the one and only Forjah."

"You are out here at the risk of Locoyles?"

"They don't come near me," I display by twirling backwards in a flip much like in his AOD sport, "you are the one in danger."

"I am not your concern!" The beast regurgitates in a growl too foreign to come from vulpine maw. When will I ever get used to hearing the reptile inside the mammal?

"I am here on request of our companions, now off we trek to Escape. You have a shift and crew that need you, and dish of maple is awaiting this Trochiline." I know those narrowed eyelids surrounding those dilated pupils are defining me as feisty, but I could argue that he is being a complete dog to the arrogance to his own life. Yet I also know he is not one to find value in argument; and just resumes his quadrupedal trek.

"Hmmmm," I purr in sync with my heart and wingbeats, "I quite possibly know him more than realized."

SCENIC 25

"Ares." Arrives the voice I have been awaiting contentedly. I rise, withholding my expressionless awe as I am brought within paw steps closer to the set goal. Miryke, the messenger of the Pros is taking note of my desire. The female in her gargoyle form is of a deep contrasting color much like a woodland camouflaged mimicking deep pine and peeling bark.

"The presages are in preparation for you."

"My time is now." I confirm with a bow before she turns tail and leads into the sloping cavern. The overwhelming scent of earthen material with a mix of similar scents strike me in overload, counteracting any thought production of my own. The forced thought process comes in the form of respect to the presages out of exclusive admiration as the strategic Taxonomist I am.

These figures dress in flowing robes where the females are in draping gowns of simplicity in comparison to all that passes their mentalities. Any of the common five senses are useless to them in detection, along with my entrance. Every one of them diverts all attention to my arrival, motivating to hold firm in my place that may one day be among them.

The guide takes me to the far corner of the cavern where a single presage, also in gargoyle form, rests ears and paws against the wall behind eyes sealed in concentration. An introduction is not a requirement, as presages have no use for names, statistics, or anything below the inferiority of their unlimited mental capabilities.

"Ares." The taxonomist greets in monotone presentation. "It would be impolite to any retro or intro to not request your prior input." He observes respectively, "Is there any need you must express before?"

"None." I summarize, "You taxonomists are straightforward to an extent I admire. A philosophy that ignores all hesitation."

"My time before becoming presage is only relevant to you. My time building up to this resulted in making the choice most right in absolution. What is driving you to the Prospective?"

"My limited partake as the retro taxonomist I am. This drive, as you identify, is originating from wanting to know what is beyond the physical, mental, and even mystical."

"Our in-tune level with the Vayl is ever expanding and unpredictable. With it, I am sensing you have no selfish desire in your emotions. Not that it would matter as all emotions are overcome after transitioning into the expansive pro mentality."

In conclusion to the introduction, I am offered a shadow position to observe each of the standard presages blocking out all external interruptions, pour over documents, and note off any fact their minds conjure.

Do I desire to be amongst their never-ending studies of the unknown? Beyond or even past the Vayl and all understanding but their own? If expanding from a strategic retrospective taxonomist is fatefully meant, what desire will remain once my mind has abandoned the physical gamut existence I have known since birth?

"Your philosophy is most commendable, hagine. You abandon instinctual desire and only focus on what is right."

"I have much in my tracks but want to gain far more in becoming a presage." A grin across his muzzle forms the moment I conclude with, "a realm of the unlimited."

"It is a benefit beyond what you would like to gain, for you will not only acquire what desired, but a far different experience."

As if I am detecting a tread territory, I immediately jump subject. "Why do you press paw and ear to the carved walls?" The gargoyle immediately detects my diversion, but acts along with . . .

"I am not sure, I only feel I need to be listening here and now. You can relate with the Lif-an Pumera designed for you."

"Indeed, and a prospective rout will enhance my taxon as well."

"Not, a question," he observes. "That is the mind of a true presage candidate. However, . . ." his glare changes and I immediately receive his mental request to finish the statement with . . .

"you nor anyone will force such a choice on me. As it is a self-discovered option . . ."

"Just as we choose to become gargoyle. Explain in your own verbals how you came to become half reptile?"

"Birth," I condense in absolute simplicity.

"I hear in your mind about a colleague, the one who is first to be unwillingly infected."

"Forjha, being a vulpine is in the presence of the one thing his race finds difficult to adaptively react."

"Your fellow dog needs your guidance. One that is not needed by a presage."

To my limited mentality compared to his extraordinarily developed psyche, the presage removes his paws and departs from the wall with only a quivering paw making contact over my shoulder.

"The grin is forced," he admits, returning to monotone. Proving only an act out of bliss to comfort me. Yet I am still and unmoved from what I have received. The moment he had rested a paw over my shoulder, a charge surged into my entirety. As if he had taken a spark from the dead stone and placed in me.

I gasp in a rise that pulls me forward to place my mammalian paws against the stone emitting this same charge. A spark I had never wanted to feel again.

"Rock is not living, as you know," the gargoyle voices over my shoulder. "Yet, much is traveling through them now, awaiting detection. Though you know something only I can begin to detect."

Eyes with minds behind are on me as I leave the cave. Yet there is no hostility or praise in their emotionless state. I want to be among them with an unlimited mentality. Then I will have no emotion toward the horrors of this demesne. My emotions will be non-existent, as I wish it to be now as this spark returns from a demise I wanted to be permanent.

"Before I go presage, am I meant to confront this prior?"

SCENIC 26

Time has been my enemy to the extensive point of recall. Now without need of rest and with fertility restored, I have only been dwindled, knowing that time is extended for me, distancing further from the ultimate desire.

Though this body is changed with a developmental synch, a new thing has arisen as well. A calming breeze, refresher to a bliss I had always doubted would arrive. The light of the morning pours over the horizon ready to bask my form and transition me from scales back to fur. However, in the outpour of this awakening day, a single husked figure appears in the threshold.

"Fox?" Ares hushed breath greets in an announcement of building concern.

"Another night passes," I observe, "without a locoyle to break this eerie silence."

"Your daze is genuine glee," he senses while shuffling

forward in a mood I know is foreign to him.

"You are not acting accordingly."

"Not at the norm you know," the hagine boasts. "Yet your mind is changed, Forjah," he entails by emphasizing my full name.

"Along with my body and species," I reaffirm. "Should I not expect a new mentality unlike the one I am experiencing?" The crocuta squats before in meeting at eye level.

"You have lost all pain in the enforcement?"

"There is purpose in all."

"Even when you cannot seek or even fathom the exact reasoning?"

"I don't have a lif-an," I remind him, "much less the abilities of your mind, Ares."

Arising in return to my hinds, I look over Fox with his slouched form bowed over his knees. I have never seen my colleague in such a position. He is always still and straight up with eyes and ears focused on surroundings like a fortress awaiting the enemy. Is his body adaptively changing entirely from the dog I have known? Jumping to this conclusion against my own instinctive logic, I blurt out at a receiving volume . . .

"Your mind is altering extensively more than your physiology alone. Fox, you will begin sensing many extremities detectable only by gargoyles. It will be your oyle connecting with the vayl to create novel combinations to the demesne around you. It is an unlimited resource only presages can begin to understand." Removing myself from the level overlooking our track, I leave him with a finale of, "When you do make contact with the extremity of your senses, know that we are here to translate."

I take leave to ready the track below as the remaining escapists await their basking transition to join me in the pelt. It has been long since I dealt with a newborn gargoyle, as I was a last hatchling present.

"Uneventful morning," I observe as a pure reptile and her hatchlings accept disks from Neon before setting out on the course. Here beneath the station overhang, Ares fills the cans before Fox steadily empties the fuel into the tanks of each cart. If we had pores, our bodies would soak in perspiration.

"What is the better alternative?" our vulpine suggests. "Carrying cans between the tanks or dealing with a long hose?"

"Advantages aplenty for both," Ares grunts from the double load of the gasoline. In equal observation, Forjah boasts,

"Is it not easier to carry them in your jaw? Does the hyena not have the strongest of mammal jaws?"

"What is remaining of us, yet with the life-force animation Pumera bestowed, much of my calories are devoted mentally."

"You never conversed on this prior. Why now?"

"There are no domestics in ear shot, and especially because you are now an "oyle burner." Fox's ears raise like the point of his horn placement. With renewed light behind those canid irises, he praises,

"Oyle burner. I love that metaphor."

"Be warned," Ares cautions while passing the full can. "It is a term used exclusively amongst us taxonomists."

"He is all too good at keeping secrets," I propose. "Quite possibly a candidate for that specific taxon." Being the beast of our trio, I take priority in lifting the large bodies in providing access beneath, where my crew mates inspect the bodies for any needed maintenance.

"The dog is a good suit for the furtive duties and obligations," my hyenine pupil expresses devoid of any sarcasm. "Just think how quiet he is on hinds while approaching for a simple request, only to frighten out of soundless intrusion."

"A benefit of being a traceur is adapting out of respect to

my training grounds. Inspect and Respect," he rephrases the motto.

"Ares is in the right. You being a traceur and naturally withholding, makes stealth almost an obvious choice."

"I appreciate keeping it strictly a suggestion," is all Forjah can manage to reactively put out. "Will Pumera even grant a lif-an?"

"You are in greater worth than any, at least currently," Ares forces in attempt to keep both extremities balanced.

"Yeah, Pumera has an animation most special for you," I assure. "I don't need an enhanced psyche of a presage to know that." At the thought of my own animation, the temptation is rising to show off just what this goddess is capable of. Although the fuel being dispensed in the reservoir is liquid, I have never been able to extend my abilities forth. Though it would be interesting, I am formally relieved to not hide it from my bro any longer.

Approaching our podium, I take the dog's hydrate cylinder, which is full to the rim. Rounding the cart they are currently filling, Ares catches on to my demonstration before I beat my puma paw on Fox's shoulder to gain his attention. He raises his muzzle just in time to catch a newly formed mist overhead and the moisture soaked exterior of his cylinder.

Once taking it by grasp, I know exactly he is pondering why I emptied the bottle, just not in the physical way he assumes. Keeping focus in tune, I wave my paw through the mist as the pleasant little droplets cling to every one of my hairs before resting paws overtop in returning the cylinder to capacity.

"Not one drop of moisture lost," I confirm. His maw bellows in a limited understanding of what was witnessed."

"My lif-an bestowal of Pumera; the title is hydro-kinesis. I extend my life force to any hydrous liquid substance, whether low or maximum percentage. It is impossible to keep track of the uses I have found for it."

"Lif-an even has an affect of the individual personality," Ares backs up. "My own animation really built up respect for the opinions and morale of all I encounter."

"Apart from that one individual," I impassively validate. Though Ares is quite skilled at his emotional control, I see mood change of the facial at point of anger and psychological scarification.

"Recollect," I reaffirm, with a raise of my digits to claim the moment, "your past is your example to make right what you could not before control. This is why I believe in the specific animation Pumera has bestowed on you."

The hagine's mane stands on end while his muzzle dips low as if ashamed. It charges me like a surge and I leap the cart lane to rest pads on either of his hunched shoulders.

"Ares, there is no shame in your doing. Why dwell on what only exists in your ambiance?" For once, the crocuta is as silent and withdrawn as the vulpine. His darkened eyes are rapidly filling with oyle as his mind departs away . . .

"Into the barn!" I order. "We cannot have a white-eyed hyena on shift. Don't return until those are cleared up." I am strict, but meaningful as he holds his tail low and sulks into the shadows of the garage, allowing this trance to subside.

Forjah observes the enforced discipline like the instructor over his failing underling. Though he caps off the tank and continues the process without seeking involvement, for once, I am thankful for the dog's intentional ignorance.

"Let us go over the taxons," I divert in subject.

SCENIC 27

To understand nothing is a path of unintentional ignorance, to the point where few to none can change it. Though this is fact, there also exists those better-left-misunderstood for bliss of mystery and maintenance of safety.

Each of the nights before I knew that a locoyle and gargoyle differed, my absolute assumption was that all hybrids were the enemy against the last of mammals. A perspective shared by many.

With each landing, my scaled pads touch every individual surface differing in make from another. We relayed ahead as backup in the pursuit of the locoyle, preventing it from elusively escaping to the Vayl. Instinctively it will keep to the shadows for greater chance of losing detection. Yet above, Neon glides with a spot torch in pursuit.

Not that it would matter much, as I will follow it right in. That description feeling so peculiar to a level of wrong. Why is the common term for an insane locoyle just "it"? Whether male or female, they have an identity beneath that unstable chemical.

"It's never taken this long to exhaust!" Jasmine observes in keeping ahead of my pace.

"Why is it keeping to a run and not the air?" I retort as we leap and glide in its path. I cannot possibly fathom perusing to exhaust a wingless gargoyle dependent only on legs.

Yet my focus is divided. Forjah is just one leap behind in a silent daze accompanied by lack of input in our situation, despite the exertion to keep up. We have the experience in the chase, but being a traceur; why is he the one having trouble?

Enacting our second strategy, both Jasmine and I communicate to Ares and Trident to descend from above and prepare the blinding barricade. This strategy requires two high above in gaining altitude advantage. I wish to transmit Fox, yet he is not in possession of a gauntlink.

The impending wall is near. My eyes catch the silhouette shapes of both crocuta and puma peeking over the ledge before springing up and delivering the spot torch in delivering a blinding barrier upon the isolated locoyle. It halts and falters on the slick surface, where Jasmine and I take the opportunity by hurling forward to the infected. Though relatively large in proportions, she and I restrain it briefly before Ares and Trident join to keep it under our force.

"FORJAH!" Jasmine excruciates while keeping paw on wing and arm. Briefly, I catch his dazed, parted eyes before a breath escapes him and he motivates forward in a newfound rush, landing overtop the locoyle. Securing it with his full restraint, Ares grips bestial paws around its horns before driving clamping jaws on spinal cord in administering healthy oyle. Neon descends all while keeping light directly before its sights. Its roars and protests are explosively non-sensical while each of us can only think of the healing ahead.

Knowing this is particularly stubborn compared to most locoyles, Jasmine assures I have maximum restraint before withdrawing a tubed penetrator from her belt. Administering the point into its vein, the fresh dosage will assuredly speed up its return to sanity.

After a calculated time, none among us are tracking the locoyle's breathing and pulse subside to where we leave it heaving in return to stability. Yet Trident and I divert to one of our own as he holds his head in obvious pain.

"Fox." Trident responds to the sulking dog, "Losse?" He glances over in the need for an answer.

"Unknown," is all I can manifest. Yet here is our companion holding his frontal lobe in a pain, like the locoyle himself. Forjah grunts in that reptilian moan before expressing exactly what Ares is translating.

"He is feeling the pain of this locoyle, as if his own." To the shock of each of our team, the moment our target begins to breath in normal breaths, Forjah displays the absence of pain as he too falls on fours like relieved from a torture session.

"Feeling the locoyles pain?" Neon finalizes.

"An animation?" Jasmine suggests. "The first I've seen, to be exact."

"No," Trident counteracts while resting his large pad between our crew mate's ears. Pumera appears to us individually. Fox has accompanied us the entirety of this night and day. Not even Ares has a suggestion to this sensory adaptation. We have no time to ponder, as we must get our prey into rehabilitation and our newborn into a rest.

"My Queen, I assure you that locoyle's pain made itself my own. It was unbearable trauma to the extent of insanity." Ethake releases an exhale to signal she has received my full account of the experience.

"Gratitude is with me that your instinct instantaneously led you to my instruction." A glow reforms her expression when I back up claiming I could not seek any other.

"There exists the probability it may be ultra-sensitivity of your freshly flowing oyle. For it remains newly burning."

Trident believes it not an animation, for Pumera has not contacted in the isolated approach described.

In the added rise in my fear-induced confusion, a spark of the familiar pain creeps into my lobe as if accessed by penetration. The points are that of my Queen's talons prickling the radius of my scalp around my still tender horn nubs. As if the one convalescing nutrient pressuring into my form, her tapered lips rest over my scalp to my coordination loss, leading to a fall in her breast by welcoming embrace.

"Forjah, though we have received restored biological procreation, oyle is unstable in our once singular mammalia. The desired adaptive control of the chemical requires an extensive amount of personal discipline, acquired balance of mentality and physicality," She summarizes.
I protest like a slur of artillery that I need her to truly obtain oyle stability.

"I did not prepare for a gargoyle transition. nor did I birth from an egg."

In a time far behind, the lifestyle performed in a primitive state is beyond historical understanding. Yet, many living mammals long for the period they have not known and only imagined. The time before our infertility and our inevitable extinction began creeping into our biology.

"Why should I give any care to being fertile again?" I throw to Losse while we descend the steel door to its loading point, aided by Neon and Jade."

"You are not required to be thrilled, just fortunate," she optimizes. "Each of us could not manifest the reality of being

barren, on the cause of not losing what we originally lacked."
Catching on to her direction, I take the lead in the conversation.

"Now that I have restored procreation, being forced
upon me with every 'attribute' that accessorizes itself to this
body, I have a sense of enslavement to this newfound biology."
Noticing her wide-eyed and ear-opening signal, I see she has
fallen behind in my overtaking to our discussion. In preparation
for delivering the most absolute explanation, I conceive my
phrases and pour forth . . .

"Although it has been restored, the sensation of being
reproductive is more of an activation. Yet I refer to it as an
enslaving sickness." Not withholding any emotion, I forward . . .

"Now chemically impulsed through my brain, my triad
perception has altered in a corrupted form. Females, mammal
and gargoyle now are visually different in a mind tapping into
dark intimate territory. It makes me sick to know how males
think and perceive." For my alternative revelation, I rest paws on
either of the shoulders and raise head to her eye level. outputting
from behind silver filled irises.

"Nothing can change my love for you, Losse. Though the
temptations my mind and body are signaling in a looping circuit .
. . is a dark challenge to the entirety of my whole. Now that fertile
gargoyles abound in witness before my new body, it is going
against my developed will and morale."

All focus is on the lupine for whom my love will never
expire. My peripherals catch Neon storming past the door with
Jade peeking around with attentive expression, most assuredly
alerting Ares in witnessing the negativity of his lioness. The
leonine leans against the door frame ready to take in my finale,
yet it is Losse who interludes.

My head returns to a bow with sealed eyes in the silver
oyle escaping. But the shoulders of my dear lupes shift just
before her bestial paws meet the jaw muffs I had taken much
time to develop. The wingtips of her gargoyle body overlap to

incorporate her mammalia, draping themselves to cradle my shoulders accompanied in voice carrying . . .

"There is no wrong in your philosophy. Just don't think you are alone in this. I admit my own body and mind exist as a double-edged chemical. Since my own oyle transition, I view the internal need as a motherly instinct undeniable. I could never feel I even had a womb till after shedding these hairs. Males make me more aware than ever that I primally want to reproduce. It's our own rediscovered nature, Forjah. We are feeling what barren generations of mammals never will. It is how we electively respond to our chemicals that are defining."

"This is why I maintain my celibacy. I will not be a slave to testosterone." Her mood turns neutral as her grip of forelimb does not loosen.

"You really are a member of the creatures of adaptability, an independent dog who is the positive one usually forcing cheer on me, not vice versa."

I grant her a thankful embrace before motioning past toward the door before Jade seals it for the approaching night.

"Fox, don't!" Losse orders, "Do not express yourself before retreating off into seclusion. It is unhealthy for a fledgling gargoyle to isolate himself. Let alone the pain to each of us." There is official concern in her protest.

"Join us in the cellar. You need our companionship to the same extent we need your own. There is danger in fleeing from your alliance withholding torment, rather than face them as you just have."

Now I am in a blunt monotone mood, as a genuine part of my instinct turns tail back into the lodge and out of the darkening sky. I trek in the steps of the lioness and varg to the arise of a calming nerve mentally set in a bliss of rarity, impulsing my body to anticipate transferring to reptile mode for rest to my exhausted hide. Even the chilled planks of the lodge beneath my withered digits are equally refreshing, in comparing the scent of

Clevarest' spiced chorizo grilling below deck.

SCENIC 28

The absent duration of an authoritative figure proves to be a trial. This isolation only increased my longing as a kit and in the present. I still remember the earliest days of being a black-pelted whelp with no hearing or sight; only touch and scent. My nose guided me with that minuscule undeveloped body, receiving her warming clutch.

Going further forward to the nights burrowing beneath woolen quilts, the locoyles were close, lurking outside seeking a point of entry. In those moments, I whelped despite the greater danger in breaking dead silence.

She would embrace me in the highest form of comfort. Creating the most protective shelter of den and dam, guarding not only her, but one among mammal, finale. The tears are so reminiscent of when she granted safety. Feeling them descend on my extensively matured muzzle, trickling to the cheek ruffs I have lived long enough to sprout, it was then in my minimal sentient state, that nature coaxed me to cling to her so as to attain survival. Yet now I am through it all and want the transition to death. Our Queen is the key . . .

My physical expression is accompanied by the compulsions of the sow, while our Queen cradles her by pressing frontal lobe between the horns of the ailurus. Instantaneously, the female's cries reduce as if surfacing out of submergence. She grips our mistress by wing-mounts in altering turmoil, drawing Kodyk and Raquel to aid.

"My passing," she pleads, "I failed my passage." The Procyon-like gargoyle pours to our own disappointment. Neither Raquel, Kodyk, or I have any input. It is our inspirer who breaks with a masseuse's touch over the female's nape.

"Death is no instant reward. Your body is clinging to life while your will is to demise. True separation cannot be attained upon first attempt. Be thankful and proud as I am with your expansion to your end."

"Grateful indeed," Kodyk praises with optimism gestured toward each of us. The glee is bringing down her pulse at the alert of breaths distributing in greater succession.

"Marz, you have exceeded us. To think you began after Kodyk, and now arrive as the superior." Our jackal reptile catches on by drawing his mate near.

"You are setting a true example," I put forth. "You may even attain passage before the remainder of us."

A calming state is settling over our cradled companion, fueled in our support of leveling her back into restitution. Now knowing she may be the first to succeed at our goal, she may leave us actively to catch up. Yet ultimately, we are to leave Ethake behind . . .

For a time's first, I ponder how to thank her for assisting what I can never return. Right to the point of contemplation so in depth, it is my nose rather than eyes that identify a beastly gargoyle paw baring a strip of meat directly in front.

"Spiced porcine strip?" Kodyk offers. I appetizingly take

the link and chomp with a strange numbing to my newly formed canids. Quite instantly, he catches on to my awkward jaw movements.

"Your teeth still require more hardening. It will get easier."

"Hopefully, our passage will arrive first." I bow an exchange to Marz, somberly resting in a reclined embrace against the hulking body of Raquel. Now I have my trail of thought leading up to our Queen; who is meditatively settled at the inlet before the expanding wilderness. Giving Kodyk gratitude for the meat morsel crafted by his own technique, I find now is the time to extend thanks to the inspirer leading our isolated goal.

Ascending the crude mound of stone, I free solo with the advantaged discipline long developed before I bothered to track.

"Why climb and waste those exceptional membraned limbs?" she advisedly challenges.

"I am only at comfort on the original four," I describe alongside in my comforted pose of one knee supporting my throat curve. "I became a traceur long before knowing locoyle versing gargoyle. My approach to heights differentiates from now, as I learned to properly deal with narrow walls and ledges. Yes, I still undergo vertigo, but intolerance proves only a limited hinder. Now aided with three pairs of limbs, having a safety net permanently attached defeats all I have physically and mentally worked for."

"Does this aid your desire for death?"

"Yes, my Queen." I admit for the first time to even myself. "I have gotten all I wanted in life. Yet now, being forcefully infected by oyle, my realization has exceeded. I have no free will anymore to take control. My desire is to have absolute control over the last . . .

"Control over your end," She summarizes.

"Coherent to the full extent," I confirm. "My conception

and birth were decided by sire and dam. Some rogue gargoyle chose me as the first target, leaving the ultimate conclusion as the remainder. I want to decide when without any external motivation. I can't even weigh the fortune of you finding me in this most desperate time of need.".

"Fox, before you pass infinitely, do you not think your focus need be justice to your infector?"

She is approaching from a blind side, yet her meaning is genuine to the point of entering my brain harnessed in guilt of ignorance.

"You can only be right. I just don't think I am capable."

"You are a gargoyle who can maneuver his body in ways I can only ponder in possibility. Not even a locoyle could outrun your traceur's body."

"Yet how can I approach a pursuit not knowing how to arrive at the point of assault?"

"You detailed you began feeling the sickness that night in the lodge, which we know as the oyle taking full effect on your mind and body." Her recall to my account plants a fertile seed as more memories begin surfacing that I had not studied in depth . . .

"Trident gave me a particularly strong hug that evening, completely ignorant of my whereabouts in the wilderness . . . alone and vulnerable to oyle burners." My ears would have widened if not substituted by horns, but my eyes are expanded in threat of releasing oyle. Having no power to voice out this reactive moment, my mistress takes on the burdening task.

"You must consider your infection may have been orchestrated by one of the escapists." Still I cannot manage to bring anything past my uvula.

"Oyle is all the same. It is our physicality and psychology that individually react, making it impossible to trace who the infector is; yet think inside rather than outside."

"It is peculiar," I finally muster with forced confidence, "I was infected only a day before meeting that new vixen Clevarest hired."

"Vision. I remember you expressing intolerance for her. Alternatively, what reason would she have for being the culprit?"

"That," I decide," is where to begin."

"Be cautious, Fox. Don't make more enemies than needed."

"Yes," acknowledged mistress. "I am thankful to every extent of my being for your guidance. How can we go on while leaving you here? There must be a thankful performance to equate your obligation." The gargoyle's expression turns to a wise and philosophical tone as I close our distance in pressing tapered lips to her shoulder.

"The four of you candidates are only the first," she presents. "Pumera granted this animation to ferry those beyond. My own gratitude originates from your devotion as my students. So, in converging a thanks, commit fully to my instruction."

"To the end," I promise, "to our end."

Why would I question a designated or fateful position? It remains not a goal, for my actualization bares no wholesome completion. My hinds fell off the trail upon going cold for him.

"Vision?" Jasmine's hearty voice breaks my contemplation. I remain with entirety fixed and only allow direct sight her in reaction.

"You going to sleep for once? I have no record on when I last did."

"More of a mental rest," I add. The lodge is such a location to experience refreshing safety. Perceive it as psychological convergence."

"Meditation?" the molly suggestively condenses.

"A vague definition. Just know that even as hybrids, rest is as beneficial to our oyle in comparative to actively maintaining." Jasmine is put off the statement to the point I know she struggles to conjure a backup.

"Your personal code is far different than most, especially for an actioneer. Who influenced you so?"

"He is long deceased," I muster up. Detecting my genuine lack for detail, the puma diverts the conversation to offer pulling back the blinds in allowing the natural light of night.

"It will make awakening to reptile all the more refreshing," I approvingly optimize.

"Assured." She ratifies before exiting the den on a near silent patter of her felidae feet.

I wish to claim the escapists as more than common alliance. Yet virtuous instinct reminds my wholesome entirety to remain cautious until this potential trust is earned.

My distancing has led to a barrier of isolation, challenging any current judgment, despite every need to find the infector. My Queen's verb rings in my oyle-surging cranium as sight takes in the vixen comfortably swaddled in the hammock. She cannot be defined as enemy, yet she is surfacing ever further from ally.

"Vision."

My name on the breath of a masculine tongue drives me to consciousness in such a reactive jolt, my hammock threatens detachment from its suspension hooks. With oyle surging through my muscle and organ of a heart, my lungs heave in a desperate cry for air.

"Traceur's adrenaline," Fox distinctively puts forth in prevention of protest.

"You require me?" I retort in total ignorance, seeing no point complaining about his silent, furtive intrusion.

"Why did you choose employment with Escape? What motivated Clevarest?" As irrelevant these questions prove, my choosing is to satisfy his urge for info in order to relieve from the prying.

"Recommended by Dixon . . . being an actioneer. Or for

your understanding, an action taxonomist. I am a key operator of various physical traits, why not hire a creature of adaptability?" My statement immediately brings up a new point . . . "It is the same reason you are the first hired. An adaptable vulpine, let alone prior to being a gargoyle."

"A fair reason miss vixen," he disrespectfully boasts in my detection of arising anger. "As the newest recruit, you have much ahead to gain our trust. Know this," he emphasizes with a raise of black padded digit, "I put my life below that of my skulk in Escape. You have long before you acquire equal trust. Don't make yourself my enemy, a definite title non-especially my infector wishes to attain." He threatens before viewing the pane filtered light readying to cast through.

"Mutual!" is my armed defensive response. At joint flex, my pads clutch against the composite bar, feeling the night creeping up our hides, preceding the familiar warming sensation igniting our oyle. Leaving the two of us shimmering into scaled imbrications.

Now the crimson creature towers before me in his male dimorphism, baring a menacing stare incapable in vulpine form. The oyle-coated eyes white out with fresh incisors barred in retreating out on fours, loosening a threatening growl. Defensively, my flight overpowers fight, unfurling three of my limbs to dangle at the suspension hook and leaving dominant hanging free at clutch of my wrecking bar.

SCENIC 29

Clandestine, the gargoyle lifestyle, remains. To the extent beyond understanding as well as beyond the reach of the barren.

"I detect a change in your psyche," Ares points out with folded forepaws across the table slab.

"My perspective here," I affirmatively detail with watching for the ear shot or glance from anyone around, "is a far cry from the individuals around us."

"On the cause that you were once among their genuine ignorance, you have now left that "society." "Zero in your trust," the hagine suggestively initiates. "Your unwilling paw-step into oyle burners is a life of superiority."

"Privileged with undesired traits, if not totally wasteful."

"Dog, where do you acquire such garbs?" a voice intrudes, totally diverting our conversation. It is an adolescent coypu's commenting on Ares uniform, the one I see him sport amongst the delve.

"An independent design both materially and visually." She pesters him to the point of becoming an annoyance, yet my mind is challenging the terminology.

"Your classification is incorrect," I protest, receiving a glare from the rodentia. "As a subspecies, I am canid with close phylogeny. He is crocuta, within the class of feliformia." These statements of mine have a comparing effect to her influence over Ares, causing his usual controlled mood to break down and forcefully yet assertively send the rodent on her way.

"Trident may disapprove of your rebellious attitude, yet I relate to the point of approval. Especially when a moment like so demands it."

"You Forjah," diverting in subject, "are in complete hatred toward attempted control over you. Which is exactly why you seek out your infector."

"A statement and not an inquiry, you are adapted to a social level I can never match. Though I will not request your assistance, I neither refuse it." Totally ignoring my balance of assistance and desire, the hyenine picks up with . . .

"Have you formed an approach of strategy?" Dipping nose downward, I collectively condense . . .

"Yes, by placing focus to each of the methods of infection."

"When was the first sign?"

"When I began feeling ill during the same charge leading up to molting."

"Not long after we ate, so there is potential . . ."

"A jump to a conclusion is not a wise route, let alone a strategy," I bark in all prevention to his suggestion.

"I am only responding to what my mind picks up in your thought pattern. Sometimes hearing one's self is a swell indicator to show the true perspective." There is a newly arisen playfulness presenting a smug sadistic expression on his complexed beast of a jaw. "Would you however, like to hear my immediate strategy?" I grant a bow in knowing there is no need for use of voice. "Suppose, ultimately, you are willfully infected. Divert your mind from any amount of chance this was accidental."

"You are motivating to hold firm on the deliberate side, whether or not true?"

"It is for security and preparing for the worst. In this situation, you cannot let optimism limit you."

"I must comment, your word is wise," Ares.

"As intended by my strategic craftsmanship."

"Another theory continually browsing, is that of heredity. What if my body had a delayed transition?"

"Even I will deny that without consulting Jasmine. Yet biological science has been disproved before. It is an ambiguous result at this point." When the street side becomes too crowded, Ares initiates, "It's time to relocate." We move forward without a destination and blindly seek isolation from ears that will unintentionally pry.

Desire is with me to suggest our point of route, yet I sense that Ares planned ahead. The two of us both had an open day ahead, with a chance of finding an activity to appease him and me. The need was to freshen my senses by making this urban trek, and they might have cleansed if not for the intervene of a musky and metallic scent. Stopping before a storefront, the pane above reads Archaic Pro.

Our oyle-filled pads lead through the glass slabs of the merchant, stocking items dating to the revival era and useless objects happily abandoned.

"Resale is perfect for finding recalls filed with every type of gamut. Everything here has a history in wait of being recovered just for our knowledge gain."

"So, you learn from the retrospective in a glorified waste

deposit?"

"Not to US!" emphasizes a voice intruding on point. The withholder is a bulky agama, baring facials speckled in arrangement of discolored scales.

"Now this dog is the first of the unwilling," he defines while taking a whiff. "Having only heard your title, I scent the fresh oyle surging below your pelt." He retreats from the opposing side of the oaken bench and invites me in against my digression to depart immediately.

"Brafstrum is my own title," he introduces. "Ares makes it a goal to see every newborn to our archaic emporium. I collect recalls of the lost, providing direct access to the ambience of many and the occasional lost anima."

"He has yet to be introduced to the contents and purpose of the Vayl."

"No better place or time," the pure reptile puts forth, as I begin strolling through the shelving of many inanimate ancients.

"Tell me dog, what are your interests?" I am possibly not answering on the account of attempting to grasp his intention. Yet what is the intention of Ares need for me here? I have only been given the term recalls, yet never its definition among oyle burners.

In attempt to hide this pondering by going along with Brafstrum, I explain my aspirations, save for the one only my Queen acknowledges.

"A traceur." The agama repeats by cocking a brow at my athletic title. After detailing about the full body sport based on physical efficiency, he converges the terminology to forward with
. . .

"Parkour," he finally loads in understanding. "I cannot think of any material relating here. With your mentality however, you have the capability in proving me wrong."

"Tracing is based not around having the ideal

environment, but by using the provided environment." Accepting

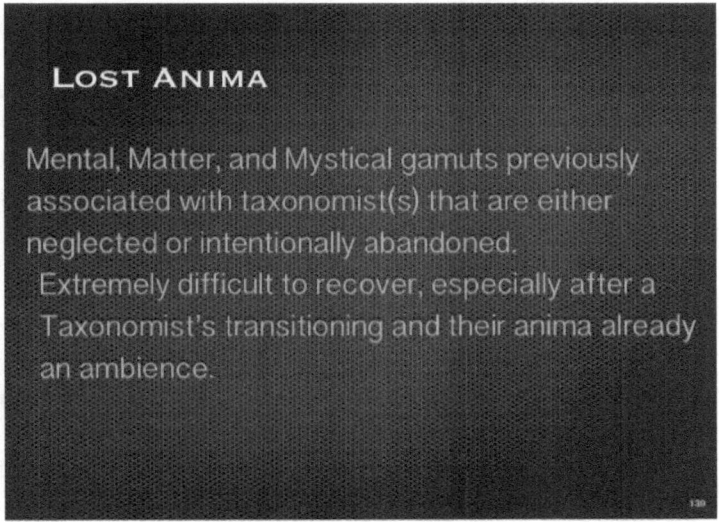

LOST ANIMA

Mental, Matter, and Mystical gamuts previously associated with taxonomist(s) that are either neglected or intentionally abandoned.
  Extremely difficult to recover, especially after a Taxonomist's transitioning and their anima already an ambience.

the motto at terminological value, Brafstrum motivates me to browse the "museum" in a collect-a-thon of gamuts and animas beyond my own.

"Anima," Ares projects as we begin our treasured trash trek," is our current mentality burning live. When we pass out of existence, our animas transitions into the Vayl as collected gamuts: Memory, Matter, and Mystical. The cleaner and greater the recall, the more influential our ambiance proves for our descendants."

"An extended lifespan," I assume, "more time to leave a stronger influence."

"Affirmative," the crocuta confirms with a bow of his nose dipping in synch with eyelids.

Ares passes while I squat over a crate filled with mere shells of when I cannot recall, literally. Sifting through the cords and casings, I pick up a blacked object baring a digital screen and a series of discolored input buttons. Judging by the unrecognizable ports atop the deck, I conclude it's a device for gaming links. Leaving the finding, I end the aisle at the window front where antique instruments are laid out, presenting their rusting brass glory of a time long past. Soon my own form will only be a vessel of dormant oyle.

The next room is a hull of low supporting beams, sheltering carven shelves far older yet superior to the aluminum cases out front. The passage ends in such a claustrophobic halt, I end up resting heavy head against the brick wall at the furthest point of the structure, in the same physical stress accompanying my first shed. In synch with heaving lungs, I know oyle burns hot in my circulatory system, much like my paws on these worn wooden planks and slick grinding stone.

My knees give out in collapse before the wall side with calloused pads dragging down into the sulking mood. Mind drifts to Ethake and our upcoming passing; to which oyle makes its way in silvery trails down my dundrearies.

"Forjah!" Ares hollers just before his bestial pads thunder across the wooden planks that would make any traceur cower.

In remembering his animation, it occurs immediately that he is taking in the mental stress of my own psyche. I am thankful he is not forcing me on foot but does right me forward by fixing back to the bricks.

"As I have clarified before, your mind is unlike anyone. Now that oyle is diffusing in place of your blood, your very thought process has not only altered beyond a traceur, but mindset of gargoyle combined." There is a sense of concern in his tone that I am giving no amount of care to.

"I am my own burden," I reject against the creature through squinting. "My biological duration and mine alone. If I cannot choose this species, let me choose how to function with it." To a relief unexpected, Ares respectfully retreats with the two of us keeping each other in sight.

In what feels like breaking in and out of consciousness, I find myself back up in what feels like impulsing surges carrying to a dazed destination, where it halts me at the source. Whatever the cause for this sudden energetic onset, it surfaced in light of the imbalance I just suffered.

Below is a corrugated box touching my hock. Squatting to the floor level in awe at the contents, my maw gapes open in reclaim of the musk to long aged material.

"DoriCuto," I boast out in recaptured time. A complete console, two control grips, and both video and power cable. I barely give a proper inspection before the hocks of Ares crosses into vision.

"A rediscovered treasure?" he assumes. Instantly, my eye catches the ports atop the control deck, to which I am impulsed in returning for the digital device from earlier. Taking it up from where I allowed its rest, it proves a seamless slide and lock in designated attachment.

"A reclaimed era," I finalize in baring the box. Returning to the bar, Brafstrum looks up from a withered looking document to catch sight of the cargo in grasp.

"A finding!" the agama proclaims.

"One I am not wholly in tune with parting from."

"I have no compatible discs," he admits, "yet you should use the imprinted recalls to relive the experience of the past player." His suggestion is most enthralling.

"How is it a gargoyle accesses the Vayl by its recalls?"

"Gauntlink." Just as did Jenuine, Brafstrum instructs by raising his wrist to reveal the opisthenar mounted device. It forms a dome behind the pad and continues with a wire connected attachment lining down his scaled forearm.

"You are not yet ready for such a tool," Ares puts forth, much to my disappointment. Rolling up his sleeve, he reveals his own set up before touching his pad to the console's deck. Now I am witnessing his eyes coat in oyle, projecting on the liquid in granting the memory of the past user.

"A decent amount of reminiscent games," he assures before offering, "I will escort you into the Vayl myself."

"It won't be your own ambiance," the agama tender reaffirms, "yet relatable none the less." I thank the both of them for reclaiming such a precious memory from being a whelp, one to provide a final satisfying session before I transcend on the instruction of Ethake.

SCENIC 30

My mind recalls an ancient story transcending long before the arcaded era. A passage detailing the exploits of a delinquent who robbed a strict tyrant by reclaiming what had been stolen. This radicle has my admiration for putting his mentality beyond lawful acceptance, with instinct alone.

His wild lifestyle inspired me so, yet there is little to relate on the industrial side. He gathered his allies and closest beasts to furtively uprise against their lack of a leader in attaining a state beyond survival.

"What is it I can learn from whom I so admire? His motive was to survive while mine is to welcome death." Yet here burns the influence from a benefaction long before any existing now.

"Retrospective," I identify in remembering the title of traditional perception. "Could I be emulating as described, in the ways of the expired?"

Yet how would this fictional figure even relate to the gargoyle? He could never be an oyle burner. Preventing myself from restraining these thoughts, I conclude, "he could have been a taxonomist, a furtive one in stealth."

My mind is jumping to conclusions at a rate proving to be a strong hypothesis yet motivating none the less. Being a traceur, I have adaptively become light on my paws to the point of consistently startling everyone in silent approach. Even as an immature kit, my love for skulking granted a drive most impulsing. It is a rush tying into tracing as a secluded empowerment, stemming my ability of reaching inaccessible areas.

"Yes, my taxon needs to be stealth."

"Something promising on your mind, Forjah?" raising both ear and nose, I voice to Trident.

"I am unexpectedly dwelling on taxonomy, with stealth proving enticing."

"Fitting," he emphasizes while taking up the cable wrapped post. "Your skills could translate to observation of any suspicions demesne or characters."

"Why should I be confined to one option?" the feline raises chin with a twitch of whiskers.

"Knowing you, it would certainly be much of a bind," my brotherly feline details while locking the cable through the final row of karts.

"Why should any taxonomist feel restricted by the conduct of their taxon?"

"Demesne exist individually. Many are confined to a single one, and it is anywhere from difficult to impossible in utilizing any taxon amongst the environment."

Flicking off our switch box in extinguishing the track lights, Trident props the gate open before making our return to the lodge.

"What about here and now, the demesne I have known exclusively?"

"It is a mix here, allowing the coexistence by each of the ten. Escape is set here, as its time cycle slows to a below average pace, providing a distinct advantage."

"How am I to aspire toward a stealth taxonomist?"

"The answer is a gauntlink, which must be earned." The point is of a positive prick, to which I gravitate seeking additional answers.

"What requirements lead to that point?"

"Showing you have self-control in the Vayl, totally adept to your reptilian body, and especially in tune with a steady oyle burn that is in your most absolute control."

"Very mentally and physiologically challenging." I stress obvious overload.

"You deserve some type of level up already, Forjah. You are the first and only to be forced into this life." Has my significance formed an advantage? Is there an improvisational discipline set out?

Blue of the approaching night threatens to bare against the light polluted skyline. The only sound attempting to break our focus now is the closing of the lodging iron slabs.

"Should I await such an offer for a gaunt link? Or request it?"

"Go with your own philosophy."

"Do not ask, do not deny."

"We respect that, so should Dixon."

"Tonight," I strategize, "after dark."

A sense of de ja vu overcomes me on scaled hinds tracking the cold hollow corridor. That time so long ago had been the first introduction. Now I am seen as one among the hybrids, aside from what I will never have: birth and choice of this society. As I came into this alone, I am meant with willful desire to see this through exclusively. Rather, who attains self-actualization without influence?

So few of the mammals, reptiles, and hybrids know me more than the offspring of a dear friend, whose image remains upon the memorial of fallen taxonomists. I am not relatable to my sire, nor will I ever be.

"You are so unlike your originators Forjah, I can't even define you as opposite," Dixon presents to my sudden approval.

"The two of them, I believe, established themselves here. Approaching such a state, I require learning all I can to drive me forward."

"If you wish to aspire, what direction will you take toward taxonomy?"

"I am capable of using my tracing conduct by forwarding into stealth."

"I approve your devoted trail," the graphite gargoyle ratifies with a bow. He turns aside to focus out over the cavernous interior in obvious scrutiny of his, or rather, our race.

"A gauntlink is too advanced for newborns. Though, as the first to be initiated against willful inclusion, you are permitted to enter and utilize the gamuts of the Vayl. Although restricted from mystical, you are nearly unlimited to any knowledge you require."

"Who will supervise and allow my access?" The lead gargoyle turns with a tooth exposed grin."

"The inspirer is of your choice."

"Ethake."

"I am honored, Forjah," my mistress expresses with a pleasing bow.

"I could not choose another," I reassure.

"To clear your mind of unanswered questions will provide an easier transitional termination. I oblige to train you in satisfaction for the remaining time."

"Where are we to begin?"

"Hither," she instructs, ascending to the inlet filtering the lunar rays. Before it, she steps to the side while guiding my paw in submergence to the shadows. Nothing exists for my senses to interact. Every sign of the past reality swallows in an instance beyond calculation.

The feeling in my pad returns upon recognizing the cold-blooded mass of my inspirer's clasp.

"Reintroduction," she welcomes.

"The Vayl!" I exclaim.

"You've only been here once. What amount and what exactly do you retain?"

"We are in the past," I recollect. "The Vayl is what was?" My mesmerize takes over in this environment differing even from Aise Shima.

"Divertingly," she approves with an approach by gesturing into the wilderness. "What you see is the collection of mental, matter, and mystical gamuts. The Vayl is the chaotic reservoir of the animas of those passed on. We gargoyles are among the creatures who expire. While our biology decomposes, our mentality and all it has retained transitions into the Vayl by becoming an ambiance. A telekinetic mentality residing in the Vayl of a previous psyche."

"That is why all here is devoid of life, as the bodies have passed on?"

"Correct, this wilderness is the result of the various animals', domestic and wild, mental retainment of the environment. If for example none ever lived or experience this area, it would not exist documented in the Vayl."

"It is literally a database for the experiences of

everything by the minds of the deceased?" She parts those reptile-like lips to exemplify with,

"An even greater improved definition."

At her approval, we trek down the hill rise beneath the cold colored trees, affected by indigo tinted bark much like frosted moisture. Though they are frozen in time to an extremity, I find many disproportional with unevenly growing branches. My teaching states that the Vayl is time layered in multiple periods, causing unpredictable overlaps.

"The Vayl has an ever-changing cycle of unpredictability," she knowingly instructs. "There have been consistent documentations by reptiles prior to us gargoyles, yet none attain permanence, and everything remains completely out of taxonomic control."

"I am in a lack of understanding. How is it any use to a taxonomist, let alone an aspiring candid under your influence?"

"Individually, there are an unlimited amount of reasons. Though it is a great resource to learn from history, the level of improvised uses has gone undocumented. A taxonomist might find where her sire hid a hoard of valuables, or land upon a game-changing discovery that went on uncredited."

Deep into the tree growth, my ears catch the pads of my Queen halt where I reverse to find her descending into the gargoyle stance of forearms between legs. Keeling before, I request the internal conflict to which she is battling. A single pad then raises from the memory of the earth and strokes its tips down my jawline while she exasperates.

"It has never been about the proper way of utilizing such an existence. It is consistently on how to use it in the newest way."

"I will find it," I reassure, "my exclusive way to interpret and exploit the Vayl." No longer withholding a gulp, she exhales in a pleasing scent drawing me close.

"Utilize the time reaming, Forjah. For it will be

terminated soon." She now goes to a kneeling position to which I fall forward against my own will, to warmly become cradled in her cold embrace.

"Preparation is limited, but you only have days remaining Forjah. Do you trust my word that you and your fellow candidates are a creeping distance away from departure?"

"Always," I boast. "The time is near, and I will not disappoint you." Her chilled lips touch my scalp in a paradoxical absorption. A wrath that soothes me to lull at her breast in the relief close at paw's grasp.

"Your passing is a permanent accomplishment."

This night is stocked with needed appreciation. I give Trident and Jasmine a heartfelt gestural thanks. Losse accepts the tight embrace we have always shared; Neon and Jade accept a bow, and I turn from the cellar for the time's finale. I leave Clevarest a written note detailing how to divide my salary as he sees fit, and just before I ascend to the balcony, a familiar yet and unwelcoming figure appears in the doorway. My sights fall to her strong hinds supported on leather padded leggings, leading to the torso armor where her exposed zerde head mounts, baring a stern despising expression.

"Dog," Vision tolerably acknowledges.

"Vixen," I return in my common monotone.

"Gaining your unneeded sleep?"

"I'm being terminated," I admit. Her dilated eyes tract open at my declaration.

"On your own term?"

"It is my desire; my duration is at end. Yet where I wonder, does that leave you?"

"It is no concern beyond my own," she assures.

"Being zerde and also actioneer, you have potential in kart operating."

"A recommendation?"

"Carry on where I am not meant to." Our final exchange is an eye catch before passing the banister to my last moment in the den.

Unexpectedly, Ares is passed out in the hammock for what I am sure is the first time. The immensely proportional paws clasped over eyes and frontal lobe signal a form of distress. Obviously the same in claiming his energy and motivation of not going gargoyle this night.

The name on my voice does not arouse the hagine in the slightest, and it pains me to leave for the last time without extended gratitude. Yet this is the moment of severing all links with those in my time.

As I exit, Jade passes to comfort her moaning partner. I am willful not be his problem anymore; an absence of my psychotic anima will do him well.

"Just how long has my damaged psyche rung in his cranium?" I exhale into the night air, passing from the warm interior into the chilled exterior. "No matter, his endurance will cease before the new day's arrival."

SCENIC 31

Two, is my favorite of numerals, as a direct connection to every divisible integer. Not leaving one behind with its measure of equality; exactly opposing who I became long ago.

One into one produced a third. That third left to fend exclusively without further influence from his two origins. Yet with optimism, he embraced and lived his duration. Allowing himself to become an entirely new creature with no connection to the retrospective or prospective.

"I am that lone third."

My paws clutch notebook and ink tube with hasty hinds hurrying through the wilderness, on route to my fellow candidates and queen. The passage I have written is brief yet detailed, a perfect extension of my appreciation to what only she is capable of.

My body transitions out of mammal the moment of passing from the tree top shadows. The closer I approach her dwelling, my bliss increases by warm oyle circulating the attitude into a weightless sensation.

"My inspirer is right; the time is now. This body is soon to be a vessel."

The cold stone of our dwelling is most satisfying to the final sensory of the physical.
Collapsing on knees alongside Marz, Kodyk, and Raquel, my tool and pad softly make their way to the carved floor, where I support overhead in finishing my message in haste.

"You think we will awaken together upon passage?" the sow proposes, filled in equalizing bliss.

"I can only be thankful for our devotion and obligation of our Queen."

"We will find each other," Raquel assures to our lupine buddy.

"I have lost control of it all," I detail aloud still scribbling my note. "I want total control over the conclusion. My end."

"I am here to ferry you on this goal," our mistress sounds from the view point with her gentle colliding hinds drawing down the slope. On my left, Raquel falls over in a position matching mine, obviously thinking I am bowing to her. Slipping from his neck, a shimmer catches my attention. A glass disc similar to the one my sire adorned, dangles from a leather strap. It had shone on me that night in mistaken reversion. It must be a strain to use, as one must avoid all contrasting exposure.

Kodyk and Marz fall suit as our savior nears the ground level and my ink tip reaches the bottom edge of the page. Where all that remains is . . .

"Thank you . . ."

"It has been an honor to guide you, the first pupils. What you wish to leave in the retrospective won't be forgotten in the prospective."

The passage is ready for transfer. Birth, utilization, and

disposal are complete to a whole with these three finalists succeeding . . .

"Thank you, Ethake."

Like the halt of a barrier resisting approach, my eyes return to the low sector the moment her paws touch our own. I go over the last moniker for the first time in seeing its written form.

I am seeing what my mind cannot fathom; yet here it is.

A peculiar feeling comes back in the form of motor control. Flowing oyle returns to my limbs that felt non-existent moments ago. Attempting to pry away from the note only further distances my physicality, impulsing granted focus to the ink scribes and not my Queen.

Unable in removing sight from the last written word, what is so familiar? For there arises overwhelming sense of caution . . . no, a warning.

"Ethake, Ethake." My lips instinctively memorize. Once satisfied, I break down . . .

"E-T." I pant in newfound anxiety and rise of oyle temp. "H-A." Breathing against the loss of air. "K-E." My maw bellows in reclaiming air.

Now my lobe begins to throb in spasms and a seizing of access oxygen. Something is fighting a memory all too fresh. Faint and blurred, it seeps into random access memory, forming in my conscience.

"There, the frequency . . .

Pres.ges . . . prosp . . . taxonomists with unlimited conne . . . to the . . . Th..gh devoi . . . of emoti . . . Despite having . . . ings, they do ha . . . morals and . . . right and wrong. However, an.v.rwh.lm.ng amo..t of external g . . . u . . . can . . . them a sort of f..se perso . . . .ty. The fine . . . ., is t . . . awol . . . chotic pre . . ., kat. . . . "

The burning intensifies with surge of oyle charging against this external force preventing my mental procession. Heart racing to keep up, heat dispels from throat, paws clench and crumple the note pad as my whole entirety joins the fight. What had Dixon explained about Taxonomists . . .

"The note!" I reclaim in memory, forcing eyes open to unscramble the tablet in finding the last written word. I hold all intent on its structure and make up, going over it in cycles of spelling pronunciation. Now, against a will unrecognized, my brain shifts its acquired contents in lead by my ink tool. The alternation follows suit and the frequency of the memory increases its clarity.

". . . morals and see a right and wrong. However, an overwhelming amount of external gamuts can give them a sort of false personality. The fine example of going too . . ."

My paw comes to a halt with the metallic point piercing the paper and soaking ink into a blot patch over the new inscription. In a sudden reverse, my oyle chills with a nauseous flush coming over like a newly acquired virus, too fast for my immunities to counteract.

My lungs find the air and instinct returns me to a memory from only a brief passing. Paws find the glass disc before my eyes catch on, followed by transferred focus onto the figure before me.

In a leap, aided by my two membraned limbs, my landing takes me to the filtering moon rays where I hold the glass to the light, reflecting its surface directly in the eyes of our inspirer.

She shrieks just before falling back against the cavernous walls. Shimmer of scales overlap into a shade of fur in direct coincide with the interior.

Her occiput collides with an impact that sends my

colleagues down, while knocking me off hinds. Vigorously, my lungs fill with newfound air in a savoring pant. My vision and conscience demystify, and something returns against the unknown lacking, washing over with overwhelming remedy. My will.

How, in what way motivated me to will myself out of life? A desire not my own. Who's?

Ears arise along with the arch of my neck to find her recovering from the impact. "Her will . . . she used her will to mask my own . . . Now I have returned to my paws with fores clutched in newfound rage."

"You willed the delusion of death desired. Your impulse alone gave us false alienated will." There is no possible alternative. The closeness we felt was nothing more than her invasion of mentalities. This is all so apparent because my mind is adept to her emotions and even attitude. The shared feelings are nothing more than her own, individually pushing ours out of the way so only . . . she is present. Why, is a question I dare not ask nor long for an answer.

Yet one fact remains, unscrambled on the wrinkled tablet only a leap distance away. A non-pseudonym forever mentally engraved as the new blood diffuses in my veins. It alone has saved my life and allowed me to break the bindings over the influence in my head, attaining freedom she prevented me from missing.

Gazing back to the figure, she falls forward in a dazed recovery from impact. The gargoyle lies beneath her mammal reversion of the burly sculpted jaw, shimmer reflecting spherical eyes, and her appendages topped off with disproportionally pale pads.

I am not witnessing Ethake; for that gargoyle never existed. This creature has a brand, the same engraved into my mind and falling from my tongue . . .

"Hekate!"

SCENIC 32

Her parted teeth are absolutely insulting to a point of smug. The tapered fangs contrast eyes to form an expression both menacing and pleasant, showing both emotional sides of love and fear.

Hekate, known as the presage who went too far, lost both perspective and morale.

At my cautious approach, the Crocuta falls spread eagled against the wall face, head arched to the stalactites above, jaw held open to release a drop of saliva.

"You find my animation a true marvel? Do you deny my instinct?" Closing the distance between us, I intimidate her despite my proportionately inferior size.

"Your lif-an is enslaving other's mind and will?"

"I use the tools developed."

"You meant to erase us by forming a delusion out of our own apathy. The reality is your own will forced inside our minds to misguide and abandoning our physiology." My throat is escalating my bellowing gargoyle throat, yet it does not break her insane bliss as I wanted.

"75%," she forwards in no time for a retort, before I'm pulled back and thrust to the floor. As would a demolished lift hill fall from urban concrete into the forest, attempting return to nature by biodegradation.

Kodyk jumps in an arch to land full weight on me. I feel smaller pads of Marz tug at my horns. Finally, I shift eyes to the side in finding Raquel parting his jaws, revealing fangs of dragon-like proportions aiming for my neck. Yet what my fellow hybrids each have in common is eyes shimmering as whited spheres. Much like the oyle surging in my own head, the flow is hot and tremble inducing. They are taken by her influence, while I am only claimed by personal instinct.

Thrusting wings upward, I knock away Raquel while freeing from the sow and jabbing at the lupine's chest to stammer him back. Flipping to all fours, I space myself away to ready for the next assault, but only Raquel stands. He approaches on hinds at full speed where I meet him half way, colliding with retracting force sending us to the floor.

He managed biting my wing root where fresh oyle spews by healthy iron. Back on my feet, I barely have time to counteract Marz before Kodyk thrusts her away to charge with lupus strike. Bowing with my head angled, I charge ready to pierce with a keratin ram, sprinting at full speed, accelerating beyond my known capability in a state I am not prepared for.

The moment of aiming below his ribcage, the six limbs of Raquel manifest from behind. Grasping the lupine like a sentient pack, the hybrid loses footing to where he falls back in crushing Raquel to the floor.

"FOX," the familiar voice pleads with sighs devoid of corruption. Having no choice in ignoring him, I take position before his mate, who is just now recuperating to her hinds.

Circling the sow, she is instantly alerted by my scent to where her nose twitches and begins filtering an aroma almost in relation to hunger. It is, however, the seeping wound hitting me like the points that made it.

She is picking up my oyle, my fresh healthy oyle." It naturalized Raquel, why not . . .

Forcing her, we lock arms and I do all in my strength to hold back and entrap her desire. Easily loosening my grip, she goes right for my shoulder to lap at my fluids to much of her own psychotic relief.

Overpowering her again, I leave the aliurus with a tackle and return to Kodyk, whom Raquel has found advantage in keeping restrained. Soaking digits in my shoulder wound, I suspend paw above the lupine's scaled muzzle which he tongue-swipes in acceptance of the flavor.

In comparable moments stocked hefty with concern, Kodyk's breathing subsides and I watch as his spheres lose their shimmering white before the pupils of the dog fade in, returning him to sanity.

"Raquel?" our sow whimpers to her companion while he releases grip on our fellow pupil. Helping him on foot, the three of them have questions, while all I have is vengeance.

Sprinting into quadruped, I forward in flight-empowered instinct toward the manipulator, who continues glaring on in exposed teeth and smug set sight. I want her oyle to bleed, I want her eaten alive to the point of respected cannibalism.

Making direct contact with her dark bottomless void of a gaze, my limbs instantly become non-existent as they evaporate from under me. The next happening, my accelerated speed sends me to the cave floor in a disorderly keel, witnessing her reversion into gargoyle and wing out the same inlet she always meditated before . . .

Returning, I find Marz collapsed into Raquel's chest.

Kodyk is looking to each of us in confusion, despite I being the one who converged everything. Yet at the sight of my bite mark, he wets his paws in saliva before pressing the inside of his overcoat to stop the bleeding.

"Any injuries?" he inquires after I present my thanking gesture.

"Sore from you collapsing on me, but nothing that won't heal," he assures. "The only pain she is in, is the beating we received." Marz bows and confirms, showing he really knows her.

"I feel I am meeting each of you for the first time," Kodyk expresses, dazed with motioning eyes in recovery from the blindness.

"The memory of her influence," the sow adds in, "is so vague to the point of remembering a night vision, rather than an actual event."

"What did we mentally process?" Raquel stereotypically references. Yet it leads to the answer we now seek, birthing from my mind.

"We were not thinking," I summarize. "She was thinking."

"In our minds, driving us to a false will of terminal passage?" We hear the tears before seeing them trail down her maw. Joining on the ground level, we all take and absorb this unified.

"We need to convalesce," points out Kodyk to much of our acceptance.

"Time is the only remedy. Now we need to put focus on warning every one of the manipulation used over us." Looking to reassure the three of them, I finalize this false passage with . . .

"By the animation of Caliginous Star."

SCENIC 33

The further we distance ourselves away from the den, the clearer our senses feed our minds, approaching full function to the point I had not known to miss so extensively.

At the point of first infection, the diffusing oyle burdened the body. Circulating its pulse through the brain in coexistence with my refusal to welcome it. Now, the warmth of the fluid convulsing through each vascular is refreshingly wholesome, to the point of the sanity she prevented from manifesting. The same arising clarity from before that crocuta took full advantage of the duality between scale and fur.

"She sensed our apathy," Kodyk observes in frantic beat of hind paws hastily impacting the earth combined with arising rage. "She took that single mentality in each of our minds, isolating it against our remaining emotion."

"The over-emphasis fed our animas while using the influence to overshadow every one of our additional morals,"

Raquel elaborates upon Marz' observation. I glance, finding the two sticking close with palms entwined.

"The majority of my own apathy is to the past," I force in optimism. "This matter currently resides in the present as it is the one way to the future."

No retort or expansion is being added to my finalization. To the assurance of our quad, there is no move in referring to the malignant inspirer by the impressionable title she held over us.

Tearing through the grounds of Escape, our dirt soiled paws touch off the earth and to the hardened paved trail. Minimal light outpours from the lodge, indicating the dead of night. Before being reeled into this life, I would think twice about waking anyone, let alone the fact none are sleeping within the secluded logs.

As a greeting most unwelcome, a squeal escapes the maw of the sow, that in turn brings a minuscule avian's shriek to each of our attentions.

"Forjah!" shrills the indigo winged creature, while retracting on advantage of her species' exclusion of fluttering in reverse. Will would otherwise move me into comparatively constructing a retort to Snowdrop. Yet here I falter forward in a sway with lips parted in limp hanging jaw. Faltering on my tail, my companions keep up in the urge to complete our destined goal, wherever it may be.

"Fox?" my title demands by the trochilidae's arising feistiness, contrasting the fact that feathered beasts should be diurnal. I long to inform her, provided she pick up the sound of the heaving lungs inside this scaled vessel by result of my damaged psyche.

At the arch of my neck, Snowdrop meets at eye level in limited night vision. In scent reception, she catches on to the oyle-discharged lesions. Though limited in her expression, a gleam passes over the dark bead eyes before darting ahead to the lodge.

In our neared and progressive approach, the four of us bear each other in opposing grasp in the moment paws shift behind the slab leading up to its eventful opening. Trident and Neon appear from behind in their feline gargoyle forms with a flutter of Snowdrop's rambling over shoulder.

Encompassing each of our quad is the paralysis of our jawbones and dazed eyes afront mending mentalities. Our externals present only fractional amounts of the remaining corruption stagnating our skulls.

Though Kodyk is holding tight to my scruff, I give out on my hinds to collapse. Squatting over the wooden planks where a bestial set of lupus digitigrade rest. It is pleasing to see her nesting, hinds independently supported, in a sense for my own self determined attitude before losing will to apathy.

She pleads for explanation while the cold pads of Jasmine stroke over the oyle escaping wounds, tender at the touch. Breaking any form of delusional distraction, the molly reptile restricts my neck pivot with paws clenching over the jaw lines of my enflamed dundrearies. Her irises overlap the near non-existent pupils to catch the attention she demands.

"Dixon." I fight the request in attempt of keeping focus on what my mind threatens losing to oblivion. I grant no additional understanding as she and the crew require none. My ear catches Marz and Raquel assist one another to the floor level, whereas Kodyk collapses with my wing roots as an aid for support.

Succumbed and delivered from consciousness, my senses give little for my mind to later recall. All imagery is a pallet of colors, backdropped by irrelevant conversations; each scent is of artificial chemicals; every touch is the fabric supporting me and the beats of my companion's thudding feet, bringing out the annoyance of any traceur.

My one inclusion of a comfort is the scroll before me,

beginning as high raftered interior, to an angled hallway, concluding with a roughly carved earth tunnel. Shaded by its lack of light standing out in favor to my night vision.

SCENIC 34

For the account of time I can't estimate, my mind is free and loosed against not realizing it was bound. I had not before seen the interior walls of the cure facility, much less be part of it.

Is it the fact that each of us wanted to end it? Is the delve truly concerned over our sensitive infected minds? Ethake has only damaged us emotionally. Why is that a call for rejuvenation?

Here in the warm furnished earth carve, I feel comfortably secluded, exempt from everything outside. She is the only one who occupies my mind as it feels as empty as in the beginning. Upon our transportation, I overheard a female gargoyle detail our experiences with a whole new side. Every empowering emotion and blissful feeling that aroused when we thought of death was implanted psychokinetically into our minds to manipulate and will us onward. Her instruction did not work. Why, is exactly what I am refusing to acknowledge. But the four of us wanted it long before. But according to the report, our

Queen intensified our desire with an influence beyond our understanding. An understanding that we still lack.

To think that all those reassuring moments was her psyche inside our own. Nothing more than an impulsing delusion, angering extensively more than when infected by force. Now enraged, all I desire is to lie here in the dark, leaving all to move on without me.

"Alive . . ." breathing in deflated lungs, I remain. "You pulled me away as I wanted; now I am being pulled away from you." My physical fatigue and gamut-drained psyche combine in taking me out and away, just not as I wanted. The slumbering atmosphere is a warm and welcoming embrace. Starting as a dark void before sparking imagery like a kindled wood pile, parched and flammable.

I see the interior of myself. The many passages carrying oyle, all leading through my heart and lungs to present the living flame ragingly but safely nestled. Now I realize the oyle carries itself through inflamed vascular in transporting this fire to every point. Finally, and unexpectedly, I enter my cranium to see into the mentality, premature to becoming an ambiance.

The first memory acting out is not of my own, as I am there alongside my candidates, who are looking up with mesmerized focus to mysteriously reflect my own in every sense. Their passions intensify to my forceful output of gratitude, alerting a brightening up with raise of ear and nape hair. We had been influenced psychokinetically against our own instinct, yet what am I seeing through this oyle display, who is the taxonomist?

Before passing out of alpha cycle, I expected to reawaken to the dark carveout. Not an open skylight set near midday point. Sprawled out, tail down, I am spread over a cruise with firm yet broken-in cushion. I have no desire to move as I wish this was the end, my end. But my lungs are filling with air and my nose is picking up an aroma enticing me against the daze.

Sliding off the cushion and onto quadruped, I locate the fruit resting upon a side platform. Placing tongue in first, I take in the cyanococcus like a resurrecting remedy.

As if this is the nutritional remedy, I feel the antioxidants calming my oyle, restoring the senses my body relies on to communicate with this reality. The same senses observing that I am not alone now, like a warm aura entering a thermal imaging lens.

I may have been premeditatedly startled, if not already drained of any left-over vitality. The same vitality for my desire of demise.

The Ailurus slumps over in her sunset aura to lend a paw as I come to my own hind. Raquel offers a carved stump which I accept and take a seat directly opposite Kodyk. After breathing for what feels like a recapture of cardio, the lupine relays against my progressively awakening state.

"We are in the Locoyle rehabilitation unit. Here on the cause that we are the victims rather than the pupils lead astray."

"We don't know what is real anymore," Marz forces out in a tone filled with doubt and regret.

"We were informed before you were brought in," Raquel describes, "that our minds are still under withdrawal from her manipulation . . ."

"Requiring time to recover."

"The side of right," our sow companion pleads, "how can we be so wrong from such a promising beginning, leading us though teachings that only empowered our preparation."

"Delusional corruption," a declaring voice sounds for each of us to witness. We exchange glances, jaw dropped in newfound collaborative ratification, along with elevated beats accompanied in tune with air being syphoned from our emptied airways.

Slumping over into a collapse, meditation reclaims me

back in a quiet transition. Marz is nuzzling Raquel's shoulder while the remaining dog lays back in a hoarse exhale. As we share our desire for passing on, we now share our tiresome recovery, as is the delve's description. The guilt pressures our bodies by draining the mentally built emotion that seemed so harmonious in her influence.

"Hekate," the loathing moniker passes out on a voice not my own. "The gargoyle you falsely acknowledged as Ethake, your Queen, has left a psychotically damaging impression on each of your anima."

"Cut out the over extensive detail!" I outburst in vibrations curling up my throat. That captress drugged us to our terminated arrival. Her psychokinetic contagion will expand beyond our corruption, devoid of any chance of there being a final victim."

Dixon picks up on my hostility despite remaining seated on the boulder. My hinds are raising me to an overshadowing glare from above. Though we had been shifted back to mammal upon admittance, the fact of the enraged reptile beneath indicates the obvious.

"You have reason for uncontainable rage, Forjah." The corsac then seeks inquiry. "Or is my assumption of your drastically unstable oyle being clarified?" My level of emotional imbalance is at unrecognized proportion, dually signified by each consistent palpitate.

"Anger and protest are a right to my own instinctive reaction. As much apathy runs through my vascular, it further impulses to counteract the withdrawal I'm enduring. Yet is my vexatious emotion at any level differing from when I became the first unwillingly infected?"

"Forjah, your word is currently an undetermined product of either your nature or that of your captress."

"All desire is falsified in her characteristic alone." My

assurance is genuine for the lack of anything beyond word to prove otherwise. Our get-away orchestrated and succeeded in both breaking away from her psychokinetic influence and restraining the sanity we didn't know we longed for.

Of the candidates, I am the loner in knowing Dixon. The largest dividend between us is the trust broken by that gargoyle, who never was an instructor, let alone inspirer from the beginning. Breaking away from her cognitive grasp is proving to be an acclaimed chance compared to regaining any form of trust with sane oyle burners. The same reptile hybrids who took in this invalid newborn.

Dixon, in a blunt rest of frontals cradling cornea surrounded pupils, expresses, "You are among a level of neutrality with the consciences of gargoyle yet the instability of locoyle. You cannot put trust into your physiology at any level beyond our own." The statement surges as gamuts in my oyle stream in a heated arise of newly boiled temper. Air builds in my trachea to a regurgitating growl, to the point of every negative emotion building in my larynx at a level of ferocity.

In synchronized instance, the seated creature before me blurs to a hunched figure. His pulsing haven isolates itself from those in proximity, carrying its fresh maintained scent to my nostrils before creeping down over taste receptors.

The stimulation provided by his oyle aroma soothes my form's entirety to the extent of a newly acquired bliss, tempting my physiological crave. The equivalent need to that of a newborn kit releasing from its mother's womb, only to be guided to her mammary by enticement of scent. Each caress of this warmth soothes reassuringly in a draw taking my reminiscent mind back through the lunar shaded trees, to the hollowed cliff, and to the cavern where . . .

As the feral of my charisma summons me back to the wilderness, fearful induction reclaims anger to the point of oyle draining from my pupils. The blurred view of Dixon falls to present my four paws catching me on the grind floor. Air refills cardiology, filling my veins with cooled oyle as I force every amount of will against her memory. Every scent diverges harmoniously in prevention of an isolated aroma, accompanied by the guilt of my carnivorous delusion.

"Caliginous Star," Dixon references in a non-existent amount of doubt. Retaining coordination upon hinds again, Marz is holding her head with Raquel and Kodyk rubbing their eyes.

"Captress," exasperates the aliurus. "Is there not a dislodging method against her?" In an irrelevant step ahead, how did I break focus from Caliginous Star just now, when she had remotely urged to view Dixon as prey?

"The one factor she fed me is the rage against her influence." At the spew of my account, the key presents itself in the exact moment the familiar presage voice rings out for all in accord.

"Anger, Forjah. Your budding despise toward whom attempted full corruption has received a rejector's back fire."

"Hekate," reaffirms the presage against all disgust, "gained advantage from what is little more than a desire. Now she is at a limitation on the cause of you're devoid of gratitude. Forming a psychological battle of her desire and your rejection."

The identity of this specific presage is out of my reach, yet his implemented diagnosis is building a relieving inclusion. Casting and receiving equally gratified expression with the candidates and Dixon, this factful jot proves comforting. The fear of victimization drastically alters to a managing level most unexpected. Rolling off my tongue, it proves a summarizing absorption of "Our false inspirer processed manipulatively into our animas, while ultimately building the one counteraction to her preachings." The strength of my declare impulses to immediately land in the mentality of "Like my unwilling infection, she planted the entrapment, only for it to become the one key to its release."

SCENIC 35

The captress is a burning current circulating through the vascular, operated in the same mind attempting entrapment. Many of my desires are to withhold in the safety of the rehabilitation unit, where I am no harm to others or myself.

Despite being in scales under the chilled night, my homeothermic body pulses forth exhaled mist. Every direction into the wilderness signals the call of locoyle. Assuredly, any form of prey quivers beneath the earth in geological safety.

"Our negatively infected counterparts thrive here on the surface," Snowdrop observes in comparative echoes to my mental process. "Dragon-mammals, as you are classified, are imprisoned by more than stone carved tunnels," she associates in putting forth the reference to the chemical we all share.

"Our fear of ridicule and receiving a quick end, proves a burden equally as hot," Losse reflects in sync to the Trochilidae's departure of common mood.

"Jasmine excluded," singles out Snowdrop in relation to the poikilothermal gargoyle. "Is your pace matched with the warm burners, puma? Do you fight such a disadvantage?"

"Always," chimes Jasmine with a shudder in her jaw, perfectly identifying the struggle even with the dawned garment layers. As I cannot relate to temperature management, my agitation only grew when Snowdrop abandoned her brief philosophy to begin an eye to eye claim of the cougar's contact.

I am limited if not absent of understanding how she is Trident's companion. Alternatively, Jasmine lands an exclusive role to my friend. Yet the avian and feline compete for his attention, not knowing they are irreplaceable and incomparable. To the extent of maintaining our relationships, I do believe this personal dominance has no need of third party inclusion.

While Jasmine huddles against the cold, straining to keep up her side of conversation, my instinct and desire merge with focus on the wilderness, each sense scouting the territory and beyond. As the point of the risk steadily climbs, I find each emotion resting uninterrupted, aided by the rambling puma and Trochilidae. Subsequently, I thrive in this preferred moment over the chance of Hekate's dominion.

"Will you confront her?" questions Jade from the side in a murmur of comforting scarcity.

"WE are to confront her," Raquel projects out, much to my thanks for saving any words I have for Caliginous Star.

He receives only the minimal amount of concern in the tone of both the latrans and Ailurus, while I trace keratin talons over the peak's edge above the lunar shaded earth below. How I desire my entirety to be taken in delivering this dog to his finale. Ares detects this and forces emotion on Fox and prevents his delusion.

"If she shows," Neon anxiously rattles her lacrosse staff over stone, "what is our first move?" The tigress proposes with forced, but genuine confidence, "Notify Dixon and all the gregarious. From there, we improvise our responding move." Losse details in our lack of a plan. Instinct is our reliance, just as the first moments of our beginning, the birth of the final generation.

My gratitude for being here and alive is overpowering to the point of freedom. The captress would have overtaken in use of her mind. Yet it is unclear what she planned, as to why I did not inquire or question the process. Why did I never mention her to the Escapists? Did she affect my decisions?

"I want to determine my end," I declare in a throbbing conscience. "Why can I not choose without influence apart from my own?" In a fetal position while sealing my sights, the last image is of the distant ground. As done in the garage and the chamber, I longingly plead for the emptying of my vessel.

"You are not my end, Hekate!" I vow in rising emotion. "I offer 'your' demise," my clenched forepaws express in outpour of my mood.

In a retracting burst, a familiar lupine pad and obvious feline extension clasp around either of my horns. With sight re-exposed, I am followed up with the two sheltering over. Trident sports his feline whiskers while Losse lets her jaw hang in reveling reptilian teeth, adding expression to her canine eyes beyond.

"A cliff's edge is not ideal for mediating, let alone resting."

"You are in withdrawal, Fox," Losse specifies with a comforting paw resting over my knee cap. "Do not withdraw from us, your closest kin. Isolation, for once as we know, is only a resulting danger."

I grant her an approving bow, pulling a knee back to rest over in embracing the leg with forearms and membraned drapes. Trident downs to a squat where Losse huddles at my opposing side, positioning in a comforting pose. The three of us have endured far longer than any, though I would rather expire in life while they extend theirs. The temptation in bringing this recovered cache of emotion is tempting. Yet before the point, my lips part and tongue work to find its verbals . . .

"ARES!" shrieks our leonine crewman. In the moment my neck arches to catch on, Jade's tufted, scale-lined tail is disappearing over the rock face. In our coinciding reaction, I transition to quads before joining the pursuit of the gargoyle. She hurls to the ground level in urge of closing the distance between us and the tree line.

At the point of ignoring to catch a breath, we break the forest edge to a shaded figure raised up on hinds with head sulking at neck point. Only the minimal response of accepting the embrace of his mate reassures he is sound, yet in an unidentifiable distress.

"Whereabouts, Crocuta, have you disappeared to?" Trident scolds in a purred vibration of a demand.

"That who is feared, instigated me to withdrawal," Ares describes against our misunderstanding.

"Forjah nearly was claimed, mind and body. Distancing yourself has no benefit, as he has proven tonight."

"Her residual presence proves far too fresh in my psyche," our crewman exasperates through a clutch over Jade.

"She, Caliginous Star," pants Marz, "attempted to seize you?" In a darkness I assumed incapable, Ares arches up to meet our awaiting expression in full face reveal. She backs away in a jolt reflecting within Raquel, Kodyk, and myself. Though these two individuals previously hadn't crossed my mind, they obviously share intersecting paths. An encounter comparable only to our own.

With my elevated pulse and heaving cardio, the fashion of his obstructed eyes and height of the opened ears recall a figure undesired. The roundness of his bridging muzzle is all too reminiscent of another's image, whom we dearly want eternally repressed.

"She has been infecting my mind long before your corruption," he pries in sudden prevention of any follow-up. "Bios is whom I deny in every reality." He trembles in a temporary loss of thought train before picking up in the grasp of Jade's support.

"In denying her, however, I am denying my own origins."

SCENIC 36

In the forgotten times before now, my understanding of the systematics of the urban setting remained in ignorance. Now in the domestic reality of oyle burners, the various exclusive systems present themselves as monotonous, granting a perspective I should have been instructed from point of birth.

"You are late to the conducts, Forjah," realizes Jasmine in her blatant attempt at hindering my isolated regret. "Just know for us taxonomists, each of our level progressions have a beginning with an unseen end, extending far beyond our lifeline."

"A lifeline I want terminated despite narrowly losing it this night." Though my feelings feed into what my mind dictates, I only see a reaction in Ares' tinted pupils. He is the one who acknowledges the apathy of my vitality.

The hagine rights himself up in the cradling fours of Jade, forcing me to obtain his focus in what I fear is a protest. Yet here, his scrutiny only pesters like points on the border of pricking my anger.

"She has laid a lingering poison in your head. An infection not only circulating through your physicality, but also mentality." His weight to the accusation proves descriptive to an over-bearing extent.

"Express emotion," he sternly advises with a change of disputed transitioning tone, "that dam of mine . . ." Before his conclusion, Losse hisses to alert each of us. Down in the valley in no attempt at concealment, broods a single lurking quad-footed beast. Though my vulpine eyes pick up his external coloration, would he not have the same advantage in detecting us?

"Locoyle!" identifies Neon with the assurance each of us share. The brute is keeping nose low to the earth, scenting for reasons we can only assume as predatory. If it is seeking oyle, we are the obvious candidates.

"It should be prowling forward. Has it not already detected our heat signatures?" In total misinterpretation of Kodyk's meaning, he informatively describes the oyle-filled pupils of locoyles seen in thermal imagery. "We should flare up in this night chilled plain."

To know that the influence of Bios runs through the mind of my colleague sickens my entirety to the guilt of not picking it up before now. The way Forjah's mind synced in tandem with emotions, proved me as completely oblivious. She orchestrated his thought process in keeping herself free from his psyche, thus preventing her exposure.

"With the physical pain of her prevalence invading the nerves of my body, I was unable to detect this presence in Fox's mind." Each set of oriented eyes turn to fully receive my declaration. "My shame is not for my obvious mistake but for the corruption of Bios. My one way into this realty, formed in the womb and shed of the shell." Although Fox is a dog who prides all isolated seclusion, his emotions are letting loose in an absorbing remedy, living whole and pulsing of fresh circulating oyle.

"Ares, she has affected us similarly with the same falsified care. In doing so has only strengthened us as the enemy. Let us bypass our moral and focus on what instinct instructs." There is nothing this dog despises more than one overriding his self-control. With an enforced hesitation to reject, Trident closely watches Jasmine descend in a return to the ground level. In a predatory attempt at stealth that could benefit from the corresponding taxon.

"Being a cold-oyled gargoyle," I explain to Forjah, "Jasmine has excellent camouflage against the cover of night. Colder than anything around, she is a black spot in the vision of our enemy."

The cougar keeps low in her biped approach, daring movement only when the locoyle glances away in its scavenging.

"I know as of this night, the need for oyle consumption. However, this particular individual is not reflecting the hunger I experienced."

"Comparing yourself to a locoyle is an unfair verse," Losse observes. "You were mentally corrupted by the captress, not suffering from health negligence."

"The fresh oyle aroma," I challenge, "touched my taste buds with enticing hunger."

"On the cause your mind was suffering withdrawals from her interference." Dropping any additional concern to the subject, I return focus to Jasmin's stalking from our view point. She has halted directly behind a thickly growing thistle bush, obviously intent on preventing risk of detection.

"Fight or Flight, Jasmine," Trident challenges in a tone emitting his overall concern. Although my mind continues as not entirely my own, I am at my colleagues' side, desiring to add support for his mate.

"Have I not eliminated the captress' only motive? Locoyles are now the one enemy. They are the victims while she remains a villain."

"Hekate," Trident dares in stating her true moniker, "Caliginous Star is an infectious creature who is a harm to even locoyles. She will win upon eliminating everyone before our race has the chance to rehabilitate."

"She would do so," Jade additionally intervenes, "only to prove her non-existent authority. To think positively, her influence did not influence her own offspring." The lioness positively features while passing her bestial paw over the jawbone of Ares, who is under a fixed uninterrupted gaze.

The entirety of my attention is to my fellow candidates. Kodyk watches over Jasmine and Raquel cradles his mate in a single forearm while perking his ears in every direction.

"Does your mind feel entirely your own," I extend, with paw outstretched to the sow's competitive digital pad.

"It is as though I have been reclaimed after having no knowledge it was taken."

"I never assumed to long for what I did not acknowledge as lost," Raquel details in simplified terminology. My fellow canid presents an equally damaging glare right back into mine before Kodyk includes himself.

"We are of limited relation even now," he expresses in a personal extension of likewise emotion. "Yet our shared endurance under the psycho captress has birthed the survivors we are, unified victims." Against my own fathom of converging thought process, the summarization of the lupine is on my tongue in an instant.

"We four who share apathetic living, only crossed trails on the cause of . . ."

"Our recruitment by the captress!" finalizes the sow.

"A thanks that can only be extended to one . . ." closes Raquel with no need of additional phrasing.

"Optimism has always been an ironic strength of your own," Losse reflects in joining us from over shoulder. We lean into each other embracing with a cling of bliss, a sensation I so want to extend to Jasmine.

The cold burner has not maneuvered any closer. She settles reassuringly blended against the locoyle's vision. Though my intent on paying attention is sidetracked, the moment of casting a returning glance to the enemy. It too has taken up a position of paralysis with fores spread as if ready to prowl. Only its folded sails stealthily flutter, suspended above shoulders.

In an instant too quick to calculate, its head cocks in our direction with horns lowered before the follow-up of a roar carrying its volume across the plain. The one response granted is an alert of Ares blasting atop his hinds in a wild express of mixed emotion.

"BIOS!!!" he erupts in alert. Jasmine takes no extra time in reversing in retreat before climbing the cliffside. Losse is opening the hatch to the underworld the same moment our audio mounted sensors are summoned in every direction. From the depth of the wooden areas to the visual expanse over the horizon, locoyle silhouettes are ganging up in overwhelming quantity. At once and in sync, zeroing our clifftop refuge as the only target.

None voice or protest. Ares pulls me forward into the underworld. My fellow candidates follow with Losse ending the retreat before sealing the hatch securely.

"Dixon." Trident breaks the silence. No more lips are moving, only the swift thundering of ten pairs of hybrid pads here among the passages.

SCENIC 37

Among the escapists, my traceur's paws are the most silent in tandem to saving every breath for arrival. Though it is our auditory refrain building like an arisen overload. Are we to flood the delve in a verbal contagion and employ a terror I am incapable of fathoming?

Withdrawn into my own mind, my senses are on full alert. What warns each of us, is the low menacing growl of a larynx belonging only to a particular species, a species to be longingly left behind. The crocuta will never again bear, as Ares is the sole remainder in his genus, making us the last to experience the instinctual warning of the hyena. For the fact of being a rarity, it is the exact significance permanently lingering on each of us.

My vision alone has the least experience among these tunnels. Yet my alertness is set off by the lack of illumination and full activation of night vision. For the delve is darkened far extensively more than I have come to know. The temptation to question this authenticity arises, if not for an instructive instinct motivating otherwise.

Trident presses to the wall, daring to angle head forward. This ominous tranquility is triggering the fight or flight reaction, yet why is a familiar sensation coming over? A sensation forever mentally ingrained?

Empowered by the cling to my reawakened emotion, my nerves find footholds, followed by descending into quadruped. Ready to storm the naturally darkened cavern.

"Scramble!" Trident orders. No protest is presented by any escapist.

In tune with my traceur's act, I bound in minimal sound, despite minimal use to the art of displacement within this displaced body. If I am too perfect as a stealth taxonomist, being furtive in this body is of the greatest necessity. Is this how I avoided the Locoyles in the past? Being near undetectable by lacking a patter? The treks to the den, why Hymnock found me before anyone else; remaining undetected just might be solved by the care of paw steps.

Yet with the combined effort of sensory organs, there is one whom I am unable to stealth against. My physicality cannot evade the animation she developed, for it's exactly how she found me long before having a chance to discover her. My will no longer wishes to attach a name let alone a title; and this is exactly why Ares refuses to name her as the lone offspring. It is his bi-pedals that bring up alongside, where he falls forward on quads without a care for silence.

"She does not need her senses to locate us?" I rhetorically put out in my mind.

"Affirmed," he mouths in a deep hush. Alternatively, the delve feels lifeless to the most absolute opposition. Every location from the memorial stage to the culinary tents are deserted.

"The slabs are each shut," my crocuta ally directs in observation of the dens closed off on steel hinges I have never seen. The lack of voices from the interiors to the lack of anyone turns me off like a newly acquired virus. For being torn between hairs and scales, my sympathy for the delve's inhabitants equalizes with the hatred for whom our guess assures is near.

"My animation," Ares introduces, "is to witness the processing of an individual's mind. Bios, as you know in my relation; has animated a psychokinetic mentality."

"The captress," I dare to define, "has greater desire of manipulation of the minds of others . . . "

"Psychokinesis combined with psychosis within a vessel of immoral instinct. Could there exist a better definition for the captress?"

"You dog," Ares interjects, "know her to an extensive limit nearing the level of my own." Regret is with every part of me now as it will remain.

The two of us peer over to the culinary tents where Neon inspects along with Jade, who grants her hagine gargoyle a concern-filled glare. Knowing he is feeling her psyche to a limit I will never know, I glance to find an equally reflected expression, leading off with a bow. Of course, he does not want association in the presence of Caliginous Star. That would grant a vulnerability most unwelcome.

Losse joins Jasmine and Trident as they inspect each of the dens, hammering their imbricated fists upon each of the entry slabs. Yet even with my wild tuned ears, no response from the interior is picked up.

Raquel heads for the tunnel where the Presages and the tech den reside. Marz and Kodyk join hurriedly on his heals before the darkened passage absorbs them, leaving only the patter of keratinized talons creeping over the stone floor.

Ares and I are left at the root base, arching up into the barely visible mouth exit. My vision tracks down the craved trail to the nests aligning its growth. Silent with the unhatched . . .

An unleashed howl escapes through Ares' parted teeth. Bursting after him in the ascent, I dart to one side by inspection of the first carve. Blissful reclaim frees my mind by a shive in finding a single female resting close to her unharmed eggs. There is no sign of disturbance, other that the fact she is asleep.

Turning to Ares, I find him in pants of a deep cope. Having just taken in my observation, he forces out, "Being at rest is far too unnatural." His statement is followed up by a purr-like sound most recognizable. Yet the noise is not of his own maw. I acknowledge that his near defunct genus always had a reverse dominance long before oyle. Yet, as with the lack of being a species since the mass infertility, hierarchy was greatly reduced with the last dying off without acceptance of the reptilian's solution. Now, with the few left in crocuta, there is only one non-male who is capable of this organic ariose.

Finding my anger resurgence, I angle up with flexed joints and parted jaws to the bi-pedal positioned at the top. Ares trembles in my peripheral, as he too elevates his heart with heaving belly to take in the identification scent he wanted to repress.

The falsified maternal figure approaches from the surface mouth, surprisingly in mammal and not gargoyle. There is no need in hiding behind a reptile hide. I exposed her, now is the time to . . .

"BIOS!" erupts Ares to signal our encounter. I am ready to lunge with savage hatred. In the end, I thought she would pass me on. Now I am willed to enforce her end.

SCENIC 38

Empowered retaliation arises with my innards ready to surface. I am meant to lunge forward with all force of predation to bear her down with claw and tooth. Am I to be joined in this bloodshed to complete satisfactory?

At my side, Ares positions ready for his quads to launch upward to the one who trespassed our wills. Now is the time to retaliate by enforcing our own.

"What exists for you to gain?" Ares challenges. With the remaining expression we have encountered upon her, the wide-eyed sight grants more questions than providing answers. In my delusional state, unknowingly under her control, there was no space for inquiry or challenging her authority. For her mind blocked out any of my logical thought process.

Now I see an extremity for the lack of any moral within her head. As the overexposure to recalls renders it an empty and damaged psyche, influenced artificially by the implanted memories.

Hekate, I dreadfully acknowledge, is the prime example of every wrong choice a taxonomist can make. Is she setting the example of the path never to tread? Is she already helming the negative in the highest form of wrongful nurturing?

"Losing what I never acquired is an impossibility," her tempting tongue puts out in a flick of taste to the earthly air.

"I am the result of your failure," I mock in certainty. "You are at no triumph here or even prior." The remaining entirety of my mammal calls back to the independence built before oyle aided my specified corruption.

"She cannot find a divide for right or wrong," Ares reflects. "The overexposure as a presage reduced her to nothing more than a vessel of old knowledge conflicting against itself. Every ounce of will depleted, every emotion ruined in false logistics . . . "

For once I am proven wrong that I will see tears shed from his spherical eyes. For the hagine holds his head firm in scrutiny to his most despised individual . . . his own dam.

My newly formed reptilian jaws bare with that familiar need for a nutritional helping that I had only experienced when she corrupted me by false impulses.

"Delectable," I come to realize in an advantage most unique to this most savage thirst. With salivary glands drenching past my lips, the drool moistens with the awaiting satisfaction of breaking flesh, ending the captress by a digestive first stage.

Paws finding their momentum, I carry up the trunk of the root with building speed of a mammal predator awaking in the imbricated hide of reptile. My bellows unleash an uproar of fully developed chords while giving in to my lustful appetite for the gore and warm flowing oyle beneath. The captress influences her own demise.

As would a pleading cry demanding every amount of attention, every nerve in my brain resorts is energy to my ears now, taking in a sound most recognizable to the point of no challenging comparison.

Crack like rips sound off in a hasty approach. Paws halting at claw point over the deep wooden bark, each point of sensory inspects every direction for the source, before concluding it is everywhere at each point of reception.

If not for the images my oyle-filled eyes are capturing, I would be at a loss in identifying who . . .
The scent, most unfamiliar and foreign despite the result of the odor, dispels a call of high pitch that could only be made by . . .

"Goyleings," Ares erupts as the hatching continues moments into the immature dragon-mammals crawling forth from their shells, outside the nest in strength beyond the capability of a newborn.

The haste I have toward Hekate is now overshadowed by the six limed young clamoring in our direction. These helpless hatchlings draw near as my hate diverts from the enemy and toward their pleading wails in somber empathy.

Only when I force a glare back to the captress does an instantaneous point of penetration drive passed the digits of my paw. In a full body jolt, a single goyling latches on with tooth points firmly planted into my opisthenard, where fresh oyle flows to its consuming. Another takes exact action by latching to my tail, an on-point comparison to an insect's stinger. Driving these newborns' hunger is among the first of physiological need, that of nourishment.

I find my groaning in disbelief forming a buildup of shock against unlikely predators. Of course, I remember, a goyling will seek its closest source of consumption. Making me into an unwilling host.

That night, all reliance was instinctive action leading to my exhausting that locoyle, having furthered every future encounter with rejection to forceful transfusion. The oyle infection has no dominion tracing back to the culprit. Residually, it has become my own. I vowed none would overcome any amount of my will, even when the full extent of my belief manifested into delusion by the relaxed stance of the foe ahead.

I gruntingly jolt at the puncturing fang points, sealed by the locking lips draining each throbbing appendage. Newborn hunger feeds off my vascular endothelial. Eyes are in disorientation mode, collectively forming a definite divide of action and contemplation. My hate for the enemy is combatting the risen sympathy born at the moment these goylings hatched with wailing maws.

"They are only satisfying their primary instinct," I resourcefully force into the thinking process by clenched jaw. First, I could not ascend the trunk for the shock of spontaneous hatching. In fear of trampling the six limbed bundles. Now, I dare not motion in any direction to risk harm to their minuscule vessels. Their leeching is the ultimate barrier separating my prey and me. The entirety of my impulsing hate is overshadowed by wholesome empathy.

In an overcoming rush of my heart palpitating to lungs heaving, I divert attention to Ares, who reacted to a goyling, only to have it latch to his pad in a jaw clench rivaling that of his own. He dares not charge forward in assurance of preventing harm to this generation.

Collapsing off hinds as the hosts we are made into, the duration amount can vaguely be calculated while under this semi-consciousness. Oyle discharging into my teared visuals, they witness the Caliginous Star burst back in a twist upon her hinds, disappearing into the tunnel.

"Let it be my end," I mentally plead outward. "Let my oyle save them in transferring the enforcement I never wanted." Lids moist, tears descend in sync with chin making its last contact to the bark beneath. Memories ready in making transference from my anima to the Vayl, flashing visually over my whited eyes. Reversion of Hymnock, my infection, the Escapists; to the deep

woodland den where my blackened pelt cradles in her grip . . .
"I am ready for the end."

At an instant I expected terminal, the warmth from my incisions cease at the detachment of tooth points, losing all grip. My body is my own again in finding the motor sensory of my paws regain to rise in quadruped. The uprising of regained focus is indeed clearing each of my senses, granting full function especially to the aciculate interrupted nerves. The warmth that clutched to these perforations stands out in my reclaimed vitality, contrasted by the fall of the newly born and now depleted vessels.

A sensation arrives in the form of my heart collapsing into stomach. For it is now empty as the mouth where Hekate escaped, comparative to the lost generation surrounding me.

I howl in that not-so-mammal roar as the goylings limply sprawl over the root carve. Mouths gaping moist in metallic oyle, my oyle. Ares catches the hatchling who detached from his pad, only to rest it lifeless a moment before bellowing with a charge . . .

"BIOS!"

I fall back in a keel from the encircled bodies, trailing my seeping oyle over the bark surface. Pulse increases to an internal thud matching my uncoordinated landing. It furthers to diffuse oyle through each of my limbs, draining and in need of pressured healing. Tense, so tense, as each muscle constricts to my throat going locked in denial of air. The gags force with no aid of oxygen in bringing up partially digested contents, followed by screams beyond the expected capability of chords. Gravity takes full control in delivering me from root to the earth below. Every sight goes blank when hitting occiput in reverted impact.

SCENIC 39

In full awareness, everything beyond the mind is an extension of sensory. Allowing every form of perception to the reality I never accepted, and only wanted to escape.

Have I mortally escaped in this vague awareness, having a sense of only myself? In reforming at a chronological level, sensory of touch returns in a throbbing ache just behind my scalp. Followed by eyeballs regaining pressure behind lids and topping off a return of sounds and chills forcing me to huddle in what warmth remains.

Rolling to the discomfort of my cranium, I gasp in the cramp at neck point assuring I landed head first. The bleak surface cradling beneath brings back that I am in the delve. The strong earthly scent and wood of the root confirm it. Yet what is this warmer scent arriving?

What is beyond my range of touch can only be confirmed upon letting my sights free in an introspective return.

In oyle moistened eyes, I lift in parting to the dens situated beneath the great root. Yet in foregrounding contrast, forwards a black set of hinds in my direction. Coming into focus, the legs flex to present the dark scaled form of Vision. Though she is in a mood all too foreign in the duration I have known her. Is it seeing my state of daze, or the reek of my oyle lesions? My oyle . . .

In reclaiming the submergence of prior memory, the pain beneath my scalp-horns institutes a bodily charge most sickening. The same charge that caused me to flee, the identical one now forcing me to quadruped.

"Forjah!" Vision objects to the danger I am risking to myself. With the incisions of supporting limbs and tail aching at the weight of my body, I forward around the culinary tents in this uncoordinated state. Only to give out when I land before the trail of my oyle discharge aligning the great root's surface. If only it were my remains lining the carved incline.

Like an iron high body seeping its blood, oyle imitates these wounds of mine by flooding beneath the sight presented before me.

Encircled where I was fed off, are draped immobile bundles. The once freshly hatched vessels seeking only their first instinct to feed, are now depleted vessels of the reality era. Once Ares took into mind what his own dam committed, he burst forward in pursuit, only to track up past the hatched younglings falling one by one.

The expecting parents shelter over the draped mounds in wails and shed of grief over the lost, their lost. Attracting every gargoyle to gather over the bark in mourning these victimized descendants.

I am only capable of motioning a touch away from the tail tip and undeveloped claws of an enshrouded goyling who should have been vitalized by my oyle. The pad of my paw rests over its own peeking out from beneath this drape, presenting a chilled touch no life form could sustain.

As if reaching out from under the tarp in denied life, I pull away from the dead paw, only to drop my frontal lobe into paws still retaining the moisture of my body fluid and scent of the newborns. An identification scents most pleasing to my sinuses, comparative to the scent glands newborn mammals give off by whisker points, fresh and innocent. Though I will never experience such an aroma of new mammalia, that of a hatched goyling is a close comparison.

Like an overload cursed with an incomprehensible amount of processed info, like a memory overloaded with incompatible new generation data, I sink to a fetal position as done in the womb beyond memory. In relation to the offspring sprawled in the trail aligning upward., if I had ears in this form, they would lay back to seal against the erupting pain of the voices harrowing over the dead. Every part of my reptile form cries out in gamuts that will forever remain infamous even beyond my lifeline.

Forjah, the gargoyle whom I hold with inability to care, is now collapsed over the oyle stains matching his lesions. This one whom I have never seen grin or in any positive mood is flowing forth his emotions in loss of breath, eyes drenched, and grunts of the crewman dog behind the scales.

"Vision," arrives my title from a voice behind Fox and me. In a startling hasty moment, Jasmine darts passed. Inspecting every drape and kinship sheltering over, without solace. None here live beneath these drapes of ragged cloth containing only empty vessels beneath.

A pair of bestial pads make their way to cradle Forjah's head, indicating the digits to be of Losse before her facials pass into view. Trident shelters from the opposing side to assure his colleague's life is salvageable, followed by the encircling of Jade,

Neon, and three newcomers, an aliurus, a lupine, and latrans, to witness this inclined trail of lifeless offspring.

There is no area for adding dialogue to this most cataclysmic moment. Hovering overhead, Vision is devoid of the negativity I expect from her, presenting the fact of at least being an ally. I cannot either take comfort while amongst the escapists, for this is an endurance none wish to share. It is as though we are only here to assure we don't suffer alone.

The amount of knowledge my hybrid mind has accumulated transcends past its tolerable point. The evening of my infection to the triumph over my captress is more than I could have enduringly hoped; yet here I reign, one of the last. Factual, here among the fresh generation Caliginous Star brought demise over this night.

Here in the diurnal light amongst being a species for a time's first, my paws make their way to the cliff carved entombments where the dead goylings are to lay at rest, away from harm's further infliction. Many additional moans shed over these emptied vessels, those of the false enemies I never anticipated mourning over as one of them.

One would expect to preside over this moment, yet even Dixon fails at bringing anything to light that has not surfaced to a verbal level. It is my guess he has no goylings of his own, which places him at a point of limited understanding. However, he can empathize at a level I am incapable of. A toleration beyond understanding as I cannot grant sights to the swaddled bundles carried by their sires and dams. What was meant for celebration of life's beginning has jumped from mine and Ares brief witness, to immediate mortal transition from the reality they only experienced through touch and scent. Exclusively, he and I now observe this burial as the soul individuals who pay and claim witness to these Hekate-caused deaths. To think Ares, her one pup, lives after what I can only define as improbable survival. Yet, psychokinetically taking infantile lives during the first encounter of her son since passage into infamous legend. The true enemy has always been the one I called Queen, eclipsing even those who had willfully infected me. This culprit remains a question of who, apart from myself . . .

Retroactively, I recall this street side to a time before my canonizing and hybrid transition. Not even the glass hides the scent of the edible substances from arriving at my nasal canals. My warm oyled paw makes contact with the handle for a time's first as more than mammal. Locating that familiar tabletop, I take up the position in place of requesting the smoothie; sending for the individual whom had presented.

In moments I refuse to calculate, she approaches out of view yet not out of my sensory detection. She is alerted to my retract and welcoming backfired glare.

"You . . ." I greet without a hint of emotion in tone. The ratafia inhales with formation of defensively rising shoulders, while I assuredly hold firm where I am. "I, your victim to the sadism, have returned in retracing the events leading to my nightly transition."

The rodent firmly perches in a relatable silence with complete wide eyes, as if I am solving a long cold case in accusing the true villain. Here she is among the urban public where I cannot strike in enacting revenge to her sick action.

"Those were not overly ripe berries, that taste was your oyle which I ingested from the smoothie." Her pulse escalates to a complete wash of stern attitude. Having unmasked the wrong as well as the doer, should it be returned in justice, an enraged punishment?

In declare of dominance to take the same control she attempted all that time ago, I slide either of my grips to the cap of the Rodentia's shoulder. Gripping hard in securing her attention, a trickle of oyle emerges over her glossed tear duct before the eyelash catches its landing. This emergence of fear will only intensify my arising ensnare and unleash of predator over infector.

Leaning in close, lips parted with exposed incisors, I bite in my own phrase of "Thank you."

Thank You
for Reading
Chimerical Escape

Genus	Species	Male/Female	Collateral Adjective	Anthropological Reference
Agama	agama		Agomidae	Agama
Aliurus	fulgens	Boar/Sow	Aliuridae	Red Panda
Canis	lupus	Dog/Varg	Lupine/Canine	Wolf
Canis	latrans	Dog/Varg	Canine	Coyote
Chiroptera			Noctillionine	Bat
Crocuta	crocuta	Hagine/	Hyenine	Hyena
Cryptoprocta	ferox		Eupleridae	Fossa
Draco			Varanine	Dragon
Martes	martes		Mustelidae	Marten
Nyctereutes	procyonoides	Dog/	Canidae/Canine	Mangut/Raccoon Dog
Odocoileus	virginianus/ Cervidae	Buck/Doe	Cervidae/Cervine	White Tailed Deer
Panthera	tigris	Tiger/Tigress	Tigrine	Tiger
Panthera	leo	Lion/Lioness	Leonine	Lion
Puma	concolor	Tom/Molly	Feline/Felidea	Cougar
Ratufa	indica		Sciurine	Indian Giant Squirrel
Trichosurus	vulpecula		Phalangeriae	Bushtail Possum
Vulpes	vulpes	Dog/Vixen	Vulpine	Red Fox
Vulpes	zerda	Dog/Vixen	Vulpine	Fennec Fox
Vulpes	corsac	Dog/Vixen	Vulpine	Corsac Fox
Ungulate/ Ungiligrades	Odd/Even toed mammals			Hoofed mammals
Capra	C. aegagrus	Buck/Doe	Caprine/hirsine	Goat
Desmodus	rotundus		Chiropteran/ Vespertilian	Bat
Phasianus	colchicus	Cock/Hen	Avian	Typical Pheasant
Bos	taurus	Bull/Cow		Cattle
Cryptoprocta	ferox			Fossa

Genus	Species	Male/Female	Collateral Adjective	Anthropological Reference
Procyon	lotor			Raccoon
Trochilidae		Cock/Hen	Trochilline	Humming Bird
Sus	scrofa	Boar/Sow	Porcine	Wild Boar
Myocaster	coypus			Nutria

www.ingramcontent.com/pod-product-compliance
Lightning Source LLC
Chambersburg PA
CBHW030109260626
47156CB00008B/2594